I0550242

SHARP STEELE

AN AMANDA STEELE MYSTERY

E M RICHMOND

This book is a work of fiction. The names, characters and incidents are products of the writer's imagination or have been used fictitiously and are not to be construed as real. Any resemblance to persons, living or dead or actual events, is entirely coincidental.

Leanne Warr
Palmerston North
New Zealand

Sharp Steele
Copyright © 2017 by E M Richmond

Cover art by Carol Fiorillo
www.carolscoverdesigns.com

All Rights Are Reserved. No part of this book may be used or reproduced in any manner whatsoever without written permission, except in the case of brief quotations embodied in critical articles and reviews.

Requests for permission to make copies of any part of the work should be made by visiting the **website below** and filling in the contact form.

First edition. Published by Leanne Warr. May 2017
www.elldubak.wixsite.com/emrichmond

ISBN: 978-0-473-39628-2

Sharp Steele

All Amanda Steele ever wanted to be was a cop, like her detective father. The trouble is, at nineteen, she's been sheltered by an over-protective parent.

Forced to work as a Girl Friday for a private investigator, Amanda is surprised to get the opportunity of a lifetime. To go undercover at a local high school to investigate a drug problem.

Jim Andersen is a detective, new to the area. When he meets Amanda, his boss' daughter, sparks fly. He considers her to be a spoiled 'princess' and a little too over-confident for her own good.

When Amanda's father asks him to liaise with her on the high school case, Jim just knows he's going to regret it.

Amanda soon learns she has bitten off more than she can chew and gets herself into trouble when a student is murdered. She is forced to turn to Jim, a man she can't stand, for help.

This is the first in a series

Chapter One

"Amanda, come see me in my office when you've finished with that filing."

Amanda Steele looked around intending to ask her boss what was up but he was already gone, probably heading back to his office. She turned back to continue sorting out the dusty files, grumbling under her breath as she suppressed a sneeze.

The filing had been her boss' idea of how she could spend a wet Friday afternoon. It was hardly Amanda's idea of a good time. Then again it seemed to be all he considered her capable of. She was surprised sometimes when the man even remembered her name. Girl, he would call her. Office girl, sometimes.

"I hate my job," she said sighing as she shoved some old files she had just sorted back in the cardboard box. They were intended for the storage unit the bosses kept downtown.

She picked up the heavy box, groaning under its weight. She moved it across the room so it could be put in her car later then started to brush her hands off on her black pants. Yeah not the best idea you've ever had, she told herself, realising from the gritty feeling on her skin that her hands were filthy.

She turned back to continue filing wishing she had super powers or something so she could speed up the job. Her mind began to wander, drifting into a daydream in which she wasn't just a lowly assistant in a small firm of private investigators, but a brilliant detective who had won commendation after commendation from her superiors.

She snorted to herself which brought her back to reality with a bump. Yeah right, she thought. You failed the entrance exam into police college. As far as she was concerned, that was the only reason she had been denied her dream of becoming a cop.

A blonde lock fell over her eyes and Amanda thrust it back behind her ear impatiently, forgetting the fact her hands were dusty, leaving a black streak on her cheek toward her earlobe.

If someone were to ask her what she thought of herself, Amanda would have said she was reasonably attractive. Pretty, even. She'd been one of the popular kids in high school, counting her friends as being among the 'in-crowd'.

She liked to think she was smart, which the school bullies had tried to say was ironic, considering she was blonde. Amanda hadn't let that faze her. Let them think what they like, she told herself. They'd move on to someone else. Not that she condoned bullying. She had considered herself fairly tough in high school, refusing to kowtow to those who tended to pick on students they thought were weak.

Amanda had left school after finishing her final year, planning on enrolling in police college as soon as she had fulfilled the entry requirements, which included a short course and physical training. Her nineteenth birthday had fallen a month short of the closing date for the newest intake of police recruits.

It wasn't to be. She had been told her application had been rejected because she didn't have enough life experience. Being the daughter of a cop hadn't helped her at all. She thought if anything it had made it worse. Her father had been more than a little over-protective and she'd been sheltered from the worst he'd seen on the job. She understood his reasons but it still irked.

Disappointed with her failure, Amanda had wondered what to do next, knowing she had to get a job at least, hoping it would give her enough experience so she could re-apply. It was then her father, Peter, had suggested she apply for an office job, working for a former colleague of his.

Bob Moody had been a detective until an injury while on duty had forced him to retire from the police force in his early fifties. He maintained his exercise regime, keeping fit and trim by running five kilometres every morning but due to work regulations, he was considered unfit for active duty.

He'd told her at her interview for the job that being a cop was all he had ever known and if it hadn't been for his injury, he most likely still would have been.

It wasn't unusual for retired cops to open up shop as private investigators. While it wasn't really considered lucrative or exciting, unlike those portrayed on television or in fiction, it did allow them to keep up their investigative skills. Moody had gone into partnership with another former police colleague, Jerry Knight. Unlike Moody, Mr Knight had retired from the police because he had become somewhat disillusioned by what he saw as a lack of support for the officers on the job.

When her father had told her about the job, Amanda had initially balked at it thinking she would be made to do menial tasks which would bore her.

"I don't want to be some office girl!" she complained.

"Sweetheart, I'm sorry, but without qualifications there isn't really a lot of choice. You could go to university, you know, but you said you didn't want to get into debt."

She grimaced at her father. Her best friend had decided to go to university but her parents hadn't been able to afford the tuition. Instead, her friend had been forced to borrow money through the government's Student Loan Scheme. That was the last thing Amanda wanted, but it would have been the only other possibility. Her father wasn't exactly getting six figures each year once tax was taken out and with the mortgage on the house, not to mention other expenses, a year's tuition at a university was money he couldn't spare.

It had been just the two of them for so long. Amanda's mother had left when she was eight. Her father had struggled between holding down a full-time job and being both father and mother to her. Between the mortgage and the living costs, higher education just didn't figure in the family budget.

Moody hadn't exactly been welcoming when she had interviewed for the job. The only reason he had even let her interview in the first place was he regarded her father very highly. He'd chosen her on her own merits, however, not because her father had once been a workmate.

Now that she'd been working for them six months as a lowly peon, or rather a Girl Friday for both bosses, it was everything she had feared in the beginning. She wanted something more challenging but figured her bosses didn't consider her smart enough or trustworthy enough to be given tasks that were more in line with what she believed she was capable of doing. It was frustrating to be so limited. She felt she could do so much more if they would just give her a chance.

By the time she was done with the filing, she was feeling dirty, sweaty and ready to kick something ... anything. She washed up in the bathroom before returning to the office and knocking on her boss' door.

"You wanted to talk to me, Mr Moody?"

He frowned at her. Bob Moody reminded her a little of a character she remembered from an American television series she had seen on DVD. The character was known to be a rather eccentric genius who had a large, yet kind of gross - at least in Amanda's opinion - collection of bugs. The man tended to have a gruff manner; less concerned with playing office politics and more concerned with getting on with the job.

Like the character, Moody had greying hair, worn in a style which Amanda figured hadn't changed since he had first joined the police as a recruit. Unlike that character, however, he had his hair cut in a short-back-and-sides style. Basic and practical.

"How long have you been working with us, Amanda?"

She shrugged. "About six months."

He nodded. "Yes, that sounds about right. From what your father tells me, you wanted to be a cop. Just like Dad." He tried for a smile but it came out as sort of a grimace. Bob Moody wasn't known for his friendly demeanour. Amanda had often felt uncomfortable around him. Not because he was creepy, but because he tended to be hard and cynical. She often wondered how he had ever managed to become such a good cop as she felt he was hardly a people-person.

She didn't answer him, not sure exactly what he was getting at. He leaned backwards in his chair, making her wonder if the chair was about to tip over. He was clearly trying to put her at ease by adopting a more relaxed pose, but the longer she was caught in his steely-blue gaze, the tenser she became.

Was he not happy with her work? Was that why he had called her in, she wondered. She bit her lip, waiting for the other shoe to drop.

"You find it frustrating, don't you," he said finally.

"I'm sorry?"

"Being our 'Girl Friday', as it were."

Was the man capable of reading minds? She swallowed, still wondering what his point was.

"I ..."

"It's fine," he said, waving a hand. "You're a good girl, Amanda. You do what is expected of you even if you do find it frustrating. I can understand that." He smiled again, showing even white teeth. Again, she felt his expression was more disturbing than friendly.

Moody stopped tilting his seat back, sitting straight at his desk. He picked up a manila folder and slid it across the polished top. When furnishing his office Moody had opted for an old-fashioned look. When Amanda had first met him, he'd talked at length about his polished oak desk, commenting on the durability, or lack thereof, of modern furniture. He'd once told her he'd spent a lot of time with his grandfather, who had been a cabinetmaker, and had once considered the profession himself.

"Read this over the weekend. Then on Monday I want you to tell me what you think."

She frowned. Think about what? she wanted to ask. She picked up the folder and began skimming the documents in the thin file. On top was a standard form the agency used for all of its clients. Name, address, their reason for wanting to hire a private investigator. She read over what Moody had written in the section detailing what he proposed to do to help the client. Her eyes widened as she took in the information and she raised her head, staring at her boss.

He had to be joking!

After work, Amanda headed to the West Side police station. The rain had long stopped and it was still cool, in spite of the sun being out. Just another Autumn day where the weather tended to be all four seasons in one, she thought. There were a few guys hanging around outside the station; some looking like rejects from whatever passed for the local gang's initiation. Amanda ignored them even as they stared at her. She was used to being stared at and it usually didn't bother her. Today, however, she was more than a little non-plussed and really not in the mood.

"Hey, sexy lady," one man said, sounding almost as if he was purring.

Amanda shot a glare at him, once more wishing she had some super power like heat vision. The man, who wore a denim jacket with ragged sleeves and jeans with holes supposedly artfully ripped in the knee and the backside, smirked back at her.

As she walked past him, she caught a whiff of stale cigarettes and a rank odour that smelled suspiciously like pot. Like that was a good idea outside a police station.

"Genius," she said to herself sarcastically. "Frickin' genius!"

She waited the second or two for the automatic glass doors to open and continued through past the watch-house where the duty sergeant was busy talking to a couple at the desk. The dark-haired woman was clearly agitated, speaking in a loud voice. Her partner, a man in paint-splattered jeans and torn t-shirt, stood silently beside her, glaring at the sergeant.

Amanda scowled at the woman's brief shorts, which barely covered her butt cheeks, and the tank top which didn't even cover her midriff, clearly showing what she suspected was a baby bump. Amanda shrugged. Who could tell these days? she thought.

Even so, the outfit was still in bad taste. Especially considering where she was. Amanda caught enough of the conversation to know the woman was disputing a charge.

"Save it for the judge," Amanda muttered.

A uniformed constable walked by her as she made her way up the steps to the visitor's area, looking her over as he passed, giving her an appreciative look. Amanda smiled back, making a show of checking him out. She quickly noticed the gold band on his left ring finger and drew back with a slight frown.

Upstairs, the secretary's office was empty. It was often called the fishbowl, since it had windows on three sides so visitors could see what the secretary, Amanda's best friend Kerry, was working on. Kerry had either gone home for the day or she was in the cafeteria, otherwise known as the police bar where those going off duty would have a few drinks and share a few laughs on a Friday night.

"Can I help you with something?" a man asked behind her.

Amanda looked around and found herself staring at a broad chest clothed in a white cotton shirt. She stepped back and tilted her head to look up at the man, who was gazing down at her with a quizzical look.

For a moment, it felt like someone had let go a kaleidoscope of butterflies in her stomach. Her heart began to pound as she studied him, taking in the wavy, dark brown hair and the intense blue eyes. Gorgeous just didn't even begin to describe him. He was like a cross between Aragorn of the Lord of the Rings movies and George Clooney. He had a light sprinkling of stubble on his jaw that Amanda thought was deliberate. It was too precise to be a five o'clock shadow.

The man could have stepped off the pages of a fashion magazine.

"Uh, hello?" he said. "You all right?"

"Uh ... um ..." God, get a grip girl, she told herself. He is not that hot.

"Uh, it's the heat," she said, lifting a hand to wipe her forehead. It wasn't really that hot outside, but any excuse was better than none at all. "I ... I'm looking for my dad."

He frowned. "Your dad?"

"Yeah. Pete Steele."

He stared uncomprehendingly at her for a moment, then it was as if light dawned. He raised his eyebrows.

"You're Amanda?" he said. "You don't look anything like your picture."

It was her turn to frown at him. Seriously? she thought. Was that supposed to be a compliment or an insult?

He turned away before she could say anything, grabbing a plastic card which hung from a lanyard around his neck and waving it in front of the sensor leading to the secure staff areas.

"I'll just go get your dad," he said.

She was left standing in the middle of the visitor's area feeling like an idiot. She wasn't normally shy around guys. If anything, her father had always thought she was a little too forward with them. Not that he was implying she was 'easy', considering she'd never actually done anything intimate with a guy.

"Amanda?"

She smiled up at her father, quickly noticing the other man was standing in the doorway of the fishbowl watching them.

"Hi Daddy," she said, sauntering up to her father and giving him a hug.

He pulled away, rolling his eyes cynically.

"Okay, what do you want and how much is it going to cost me?"

She fluttered her eyelashes at him.

"Daddy, do you really think I just came up here for that? Maybe I just wanted to spend some time with my dad."

He snorted. "Yeah, pigs might fly."

Amanda heard a definite snort from the other man. She glanced over at him but he pretended to be absorbed in looking through some files on Kerry's desk.

She nudged her father, hoping he would take the hint and let her into the secured area of the station so they could talk in his office. He sighed and wrapped one hand around her elbow.

"All right, come on. But behave yourself." She shot him an innocent look.

"Moi? I'm a perfect angel," she replied.

He snorted again. "Yeah, uh-huh." He pushed her in the direction of the door and used his keycard to unlock it.

Amanda followed him through the bullpen down to his office. Her father had been a detective in the Criminal Investigation Branch for almost twenty years and had been assigned his own office when he was promoted to detective sergeant five years earlier. He had worked hard to earn his position and his colleagues respected him for it.

Peter Steele was fair-haired like his daughter, with high cheekbones which spoke of his Slavic ancestry. Like some of the early settlers of this part of the huge city where they lived, Peter's ancestors had come from a region in Eastern Europe once known as Dalmatia. Since the fall of Communism, the area had been divided, its peoples caught up in the midst of a civil war between Croatians and Serbs.

From what Amanda had learned about her family, her ancestors had left Eastern Europe decades before the conflict, buying several acres of land and growing grapes. The land which had once been the vineyard had long since been subdivided and become a growing suburb.

Amanda sprawled casually in the chair opposite her father's.

"Sooo, who was that?' she asked, trying to sound casual.

Her father, as usual, was neither stupid nor blind.

"That's Jim. He just transferred here a few weeks ago. And don't even think about it."

"Think about what?"

"Amanda ..." he said warningly.

"Oh come on, Dad. I'm not looking to date the guy. I just thought he was good-looking, that's all."

He shook his head. "Just no."

She sighed. "Fine. Excuse me for living!"

He leaned over his desk and smiled at her.

"You can't fool me, my girl. I know you too well."

"Uh yeah, hello? You raised me. So, you know, this is all your fault."

He raised an eyebrow at her. "How is this my fault?"

"You taught me to be independent, not be afraid to pursue my own interests, yadda yadda ..."

"And that translates to you flirting with every eligible male in sight how?" he asked.

"Oh, so he's single, is he?"

Her father groaned, rubbing a hand over his face.

"I might as well shoot myself in the foot," he said. "Torture would be easier to handle than my own daughter."

Amanda grinned. "Aw, don't worry Daddy. I won't tell."

He pointed a long finger at her. "You, my girl, are going to be in for a rude awakening one of these days."

She shook her head. Her father had made sure she had taken martial arts lessons from a young age and she was confident she was smart enough not to get herself into anything she couldn't handle. Not that he really meant that, she was sure. Speaking of trouble, she thought.

"Uh, Dad," she said, her gaze suddenly serious. "There's something I need to talk to you about."

He frowned. "How bad is it?"

"Well, I guess that depends on your point of view."

He pinched his bottom lip, then sat back.

"This is about the assignment your boss wants you to take, isn't it?"

She stared at him, surprised. "Uh, how did you know?"

"He called me earlier, asking me if I thought this was something you could handle. I told him that was ultimately up to you."

"Do you think I can handle it?" she asked, feeling slightly uncertain and wondering if her father doubted her ability as well.

"Amanda, honey, it's not my decision. You've always said you wanted to be a cop. I know this is not the same, but it's better than sitting around feeling bored and frustrated."

She looked guiltily at her father. Was it really that noticeable around the office?

"I just … why couldn't the client have got a cop to do it?"

Peter smiled, nodding in understanding.

"Well, it makes sense to me. A cop would stand out too much. By the time a police recruit starts work, they've been through weeks of intensive training. They'd stick out like a sore thumb."

Well, that actually did sound logical, not that it was going to help her come to a decision.

"Honey, all I'm saying is, read over the information Bob gave you and think it over. Don't make any sudden decisions."

She nodded. "Yeah. Okay. Thanks Dad."

He smiled. "Think of it as a challenge," he said. "But if you want my two cents' worth, I think you're more than up to it."

Amanda smiled back at him, glad for his support at least. He glanced at the pile of folders on his desk and moaned. He pushed his chair back from the desk.

"Ugh, I don't feel like doing any paperwork," he said. "It's Friday afternoon. Coming for a drink?"

"Sure," she said, getting up from the chair and following him out of the office.

They made their way through the CIB bullpen and along the corridor to the main door leading to the police bar. They passed a few uniformed officers as they went but none of them were concerned with her presence. They were used to Amanda coming and going, since she'd been a regular visitor from the moment she could walk.

Just as she was about to step through the door, someone stepped in her way, practically shoving her into the wall. Amanda hit the frame, hissing in pain. She might be fit, but still bruised easily due to her slender frame.

"Ow! Geez, blind much?" she asked.

The man looked down at her. "Oh, sorry," he said, not sounding sincere at all. "Didn't see you there."

She rubbed her shoulder and glared up at him. Jim, she thought. He had to be at least six four or five, which gave him around eight inches more on her. Amanda wasn't used to having to practically crane her neck to look at guys.

"Yeah, I'll bet," she said with a growl. Her father grasped her arm and pulled gently but firmly.

"Amanda, honey, no need to get all riled up. He just didn't see you, that's all."

She made a face at her father but let him pull her into the room, but not before shooting the other man a petulant scowl. Jim's expression was neutral as he followed them.

A few of the officers chatting around the tables greeted her and she paused, letting her father order himself a drink at the bar before going to find another table.

"Hey kid," Jonesy, a uniformed senior constable said. He was what her father liked to call a lifer. He'd been a cop for close on forty years and had never once thought about doing anything else.

"Hey Jonesy," she said. "How was your holiday?"

He scowled, his forehead wrinkling in disgust. He ran a hand through his curly silver hair, tousling it, making it messier than usual.

"Hmph, don't ask. Spent half of it hanging over the goddamn railing."

Amanda snickered. Jonesy and his wife Shelley had decided to take a second honeymoon for their thirtieth wedding anniversary. Their two children had contributed to a two-week cruise of the Pacific.

It sounded like Jonesy had been seasick most of the cruise.

"But you had a good time though, right?"

He cracked a grin. "Yeah. I'll be in Shelley's good books for, oh, about a month, I guess."

Amanda laughed and patted the man's shoulder. He was forever bickering with his wife, which made people often wonder how they had managed to stay together for thirty years. Amanda's theory was that it was the bickering that kept them going.

She wandered over to the bar and waited for her turn to order. Unlike other bars, this was more like a social club. Members of the committee took it in turns to man the bar and serve drinks, which were reasonably priced. Profits usually went to police association fundraising.

She grinned at the woman serving on the bar.

"Hey Margie," she said.

While Margie wasn't a sworn member of the staff, she was another 'lifer' who had worked at the station for a little longer than Amanda's father.

"What can I get you, honey?" she asked with a smile.

"Hmm, Vodka Cruiser?" she replied, nodding her head to the cabinet of the 'Ready to Drink' brand of drinks.

Margie snorted in amusement. "Big spender," she said. "What flavour?"

"Raspberry."

The older woman turned and perused the contents of the cabinet, clearly looking for the bottle. She turned back.

"Sorry, no raspberry. Orange?" Amanda nodded.

"Are you old enough to drink?" a voice said beside her.

Amanda snorted, glancing at the man and rolling her eyes.

"Go away," she said.

Jim looked at her and smirked. "You do know you're in a room full of cops."

"And Margie's known me since I was a baby," she said, sniffing disdainfully.

"Like that's a ringing endorsement," he replied rudely. He nodded at Margie. "Beer?" he asked tersely, practically nudging Amanda out of the way.

Margie glared at him. "You're new around here, Detective Andersen, so I will give you a break. But FYI? You wait your friggin' turn!" Margie handed Amanda a bottle of orange flavoured Vodka Cruiser. "Here you go, honey," she said with a smile and a further glare at Jim.

Amanda dug in her pants pocket for some coins, then smacked her forehead. She'd left her bag in her father's office.

"Damn it!" she said.

Some coins dropped on the counter. Amanda looked at the detective in surprise.

"Uh, thanks."

He shrugged. "Not like it was going to break the bank. Can I get my beer now, Margie?" he demanded, pointedly ignoring Amanda.

"Rude much?" Amanda complained. Jim continued to ignore her. Amanda gripped her bottle tightly, picturing herself throwing the drink in his face. Not that it would have the same effect as if it had come from a glass. She could have poured it over his head, but then that would have just been a waste of a good drink.

Her father grinned as she approached his table.

"Don't say I didn't warn you," he said, chuckling.

"Shut up, Dad," she replied.

He turned to his friend, a detective who had transferred in about a year ago.

"Kids," he said. "Can't live with 'em ..."

She snorted at her father. "Well I don't live with you, Dad. So don't even finish that sentence."

He smirked at her and sipped his beer. She sighed and shook her head before turning to glare at the jer ... detective as he went to sit on one of the couches among a group of younger cops. He caught her watching and raised his glass, a smug grin on his face.

Chapter Two

Jim grinned as Amanda turned away, looking like she had sniffed something unpalatable. He turned to his colleagues, listening in to their chatter without contributing. They were talking politics, which bored him, but he decided it was better than trying to flirt with the little princess.

He wondered if the blonde's father knew she was called that behind his back. He glanced at the detective sergeant, who was clearly exchanging barbs with his daughter. Some sixth sense had him looking up at Jim with a pensive expression before turning back to his daughter.

Yeah, he knew, Jim thought. A station this small he had to know.

The first thing Jim had been warned about when he'd transferred to the station was the boss' daughter. According to his colleagues, Peter had raised Amanda as a single father when his wife had left. Amanda had been eight. The girl was spoiled and clearly very full of herself.

Pretty though, Jim thought, then mentally smacked himself. The last thing he needed was to have an attraction to the girl, and not just because she was the sarge's daughter. Jim had been out with a lot of girls, and most of them had been just as over-confident in themselves, just as arrogant as Amanda. Which for him meant trouble.

He had been based in the capital for a few years, right after he had left police college, finishing the course in the top five of recruits. While he had liked working the beat as a uniformed cop, Jim had always had ambitions of being a detective and he had observed his colleagues in the CIB as they went about their jobs, taking mental notes. In his off-duty hours, he spent considerable time studying the papers he needed to qualify as a detective.

His parents, or rather his dad and stepmum, had worried that he might be spending far too much time studying and not enough time out with friends. Jim had made an effort to socialise, knowing that there was a good chance he would hear about things going on that might help him in his job. His father, a retired police officer himself, had told him it would also help in any bid for promotion to show himself as a well-rounded individual. Jim would go running with a local harriers club when he wasn't working and worked on a voluntary basis with a local charity. That was enough to demonstrate himself as 'well-rounded', he'd decided.

He had had a couple of girlfriends, but neither one of them had been serious relationships. Not to the point where he'd considered marriage. Still, they had both been comfortable in their own skin but not so over-confident as to be arrogant.

The conversation around him turned to trivial things and he listened, occasionally interjecting whilst keeping an eye on Amanda, who had gone up to the bar to get a second drink. He suppressed the urge to roll his eyes as she once again ordered an RTD. Those drinks were mostly sugar, he thought. Then again, again, Amanda was fairly slender with an athletic rather than a curvy figure and looked as if she kept herself fit.

Jim's attention turned to Isabel Dumont. She was a year younger than him and had only just qualified as a detective.

"So Jim, what made you transfer up here?" she asked.

He shrugged. "They had a spot open and I took it."

"No, seriously," she said, practically fluttering her eyelashes at him. Her blue eyes were sparkling, so he knew she wasn't serious about the flirting. She was dating someone who worked in PR, or so he'd heard on the grapevine.

"I guess I just wanted to see what it was like up here," he said, refusing to commit to an actual answer. She looked disappointed, but didn't call him on it.

"Have you found a decent place yet?" Ben Bradley asked. Jim frowned at him. He'd heard that Ben was a distant relative of a former politician, but hadn't been able to confirm that.

"Uh, no," he said. "I'm still looking though."

When he'd first transferred a few weeks earlier, he'd moved in with a young couple who were living together and were supposedly engaged, but didn't seem too concerned with getting married. They had bought a new house in one of the newly developed suburbs. It was one of the few that had actually been completed and the couple had moved in while other houses were still in the middle of construction.

It had felt a little disconcerting to Jim, who had flatted with other cops in an old villa in the capital. Villas in Wellington, the ones he'd lived in anyway, tended to be in a bad state of repair. Given that the city sat on a major fault line, it wasn't unusual to see cracks in the walls and in the foundation. Jim could live with that, but he couldn't stand the draughty rooms. Especially when Wellington was notorious for its gale-force winds that often blew in via the Cook Strait.

The move had been a dramatic change, not just in the fact that he had gone from one big city to a suburban station within another big city. Here, he felt a little like a small-town boy seeking out his fortune in the big smoke. Or rather like a fish out of water. His new living arrangement was hardly a palace but it was still rather a novelty living in a brand-new house, where he was terrified of making a wrong move in case he damaged something.

That wasn't the only thing about it that felt off to him. Jim felt like a third wheel with the couple, who were very social and tended to hold parties every other weekend. It didn't help that Jim had been rostered on to work late his first couple of weeks and he'd been more than a little irritated when they had thrown a party the first weekend.

Shaking off the distracting thoughts, he glanced over to see that Amanda had left the room and returned with a small backpack which looked like leather but was probably vinyl. The zipper in the top front pocket appeared to be broken, the bag itself worn. Amanda bent and kissed her father on the cheek clearly saying goodbye.

Good girl, he thought. She had only had a couple of drinks, which indicated she was at least sensible about it.

Her pants became a little tighter as she bent, showing firm butt cheeks. Jim didn't know if she was doing it intentionally, but he doubted it. The girl might think she was shit hot, but he didn't think she would be that brazen.

He heard a low whistle and glanced at the culprit. Stu, he thought. The senior constable had been at police college at the same time Jim was and had had a reputation with the opposite sex. The man had continually bragged about his 'conquests'.

"What I wouldn't give to have a piece of that ass," Stu muttered, just loud enough for Jim to hear.

Jim glared at him. "I would shut up if I were you," he said. "Especially because she's the boss' daughter."

The senior constable, a tall man with ginger-blond hair, glared back at him.

"Maybe your boss, but not mine," he said, reminding Jim that there were different senior officers running each department.

"Still, you could have a little decency. She's just a kid."

"She's nineteen."

Jim rolled his eyes. "Like I said. Just a kid."

The other man scowled. "What do you know? Didn't I see you flirting with her earlier?"

"I wasn't flirting with her," he replied in a low voice as Amanda walked past him. She glowered at him, making him wonder if she had heard the conversation. "I don't even like the girl."

"Yeah, right," his uniformed colleague snorted. "If you don't like her, why are you defending her?"

Jim looked away. Damn it, he thought. The man did have a point.

He noticed his boss shoot him a look and frowned, wondering what that was all about. The sarge got to his feet, then headed over to where Jim was sitting.

"Andersen, could I see you in my office?" His tone was firm and expectant, but not unfriendly. That didn't stop Stu Dawson from making some idiotic comment.

Jim swallowed, then nodded. "Sure, boss."

He followed the older man out and back along the corridor through the bullpen. Peter stood at the open door of his office, clearly expecting Jim to precede him inside.

"Uh, boss?"

"Sorry," Peter said. "I thought we should have a private conversation without Dawson listening in."

"Uh, yeah, he's always been a bit of a shit-stirrer."

"He's a good cop, but a lousy human being," Peter replied, snickering.

Jim relaxed, thinking if his boss was smiling it couldn't be that bad. The detective-sergeant sat down at his desk.

"So, that was my daughter."

"She's, uh, spirited," Jim replied.

"Let's not forget spoiled," Peter said ruefully. "It's just been her and I since her mother left and I'm afraid I've let her get away with a lot of things."

Jim shrugged. "That's understandable, sir."

His boss sighed and shrugged.

"Amanda's a smart girl, but like any teenager, thinks she's invincible."

"What? Does she have superpowers?" he said, cracking a grin.

"I'm sure she thinks so," his boss replied with a snort. "Anyway, she works for a private investigator in town. Moody and Knight. Bob Moody's an old mate of mine. He used to be a cop but retired and got his licence as a p.i."

Jim listened, wondering what that had to do with him. Peter went on, telling him the agency mostly covered cheating spouses and missing persons cases. Amanda had been working as an assistant for the two investigators for the past six months. She had applied to police college but had been turned down.

Jim guessed Amanda had been sheltered most of her life. It wasn't her father's fault, he thought. It could be said that a police officer could meet people at the best moment and the worst moment of their lives. Jim had certainly seen a lot of it, from a baby being born on the side of the highway to the scene of a grisly homicide.

His father had chosen to leave the force after he'd seen one too many murders. Eric often talked about life twenty or thirty years earlier when a homicide was rare. Now it seemed there was one almost every week.

Jim considered himself lucky for having been raised in New Zealand, where the violent crime rate per capita was nowhere near as bad as other countries. Still, one violent crime was one too many. Jim couldn't blame Amanda's father for wanting to protect his daughter from that.

Peter finally got to the point of the conversation.

"Bob has been hired by a local high school principal," he said.

Jim frowned, wondering what could be going on at a school that a private investigator needed to be involved. "To do what?"

"Investigate the drug culture within the school. He thought a private investigator might be able to go where a cop can't."

Jim frowned at his boss. "As in ...?"

"As in getting in among the students. Finding out who the supplier is."

"Why doesn't he want the police involved?"

"The last time the school called us in to do locker searches, some of the parents got involved. They went to the school board and threatened to take them to court claiming the principal had violated the kids' rights. Some of the parents are powerful people. They managed to get the principal fired. The new principal doesn't want the same kind of debacle, hence the decision to hire a p.i."

To quote an old movie cliché, Jim thought, I've got a bad feeling about this.

"I'm not going to like this, am I?"

"Bob decided to approach Amanda and see if she would be interested in helping with the case. He asked for my opinion and I told him it wasn't up to me."

"He wants Amanda to go to this school, as a student? Boss, I don't mean to overstep my bounds here, but are you sure she can handle something like this?"

"If Amanda wants to be a cop, then she needs to learn how to conduct an investigation," Peter replied. "Like I said, she's smart. She needs a challenge like this."

Jim seriously doubted Amanda would be able to meet that challenge. Maybe he had only just met the girl, but she hadn't exactly made a favourable first impression. She was too arrogant, too sure of herself, and far too young, in his opinion.

Logically, he knew a cop wouldn't nearly have as much luck in getting information out of the students. By the time they finished police college, they would have had a healthy dose of cynicism on top of the lessons they'd learnt. Perhaps that had been the principal's way of thinking.

Or else they'd watched far too much eighties television, Jim thought with a snort, reminded of a series which centred around baby-faced cops working undercover in high schools.

"What do you want me to do?"

"I need someone to keep an eye on things. Act as her liaison. I'm not saying things will go south, but … just in case."

Oh great, he thought.

"Jim, I need someone I can trust. I don't want to ask someone like Dawson, who will just see it as an opportunity to try to get into my daughter's pants."

Jim stared at his boss, who smirked.

"You can call me old, but you can't call me stupid," he said, quoting a line from a television ad that had been fairly popular a few years ago.

Jim wondered if the older man had heard some of the conversation between him and Dawson. It certainly seemed likely, given his remark.

Okay," he said. "I'll do it."

I just know I'm going to regret this, he told himself silently.

Chapter Three

"You're kidding me right?" Amanda stared dejectedly at her reflection in the long mirror. She'd had to wear a school uniform the first time around but that had consisted of a plain blue pleated skirt and jumper in the same colour with the school insignia over the left breast. While definitely not stylish, it had at least been passable.

This, however … she thought, scowling as she pulled up the skirt. It hung shapelessly to just below her knees and sagged at the hemline, as if whoever had worn it last had constantly pulled at the fabric to stretch it. To top it off, the wool blend irritated her. Amanda had never particularly been sensitive but she was allergic to some laundry detergents.

"It's the uniform the school board of trustees voted for," the principal replied, watching her with a neutral expression. "They don't want the girls wearing anything that could be seen as, well, a temptation."

She looked askance at him, canting her head and raising an eyebrow. The last thing she wanted to do was get into an argument with the man about the unfairness of making teenage girls responsible for teenage boy hormones, considering he was now her client, but that didn't stop her from glaring at him with derision.

He was an attractive man, probably about twice her age. Nowhere near as good-looking as the detective she'd met on Friday, Amanda thought, but still very attractive with sandy blond hair and an athletic build. He wore gold-rimmed spectacles which added character to his good looks.

The moment her boss had introduced her, the educator had looked her up and down with an appreciative gaze. He had seemed a little dubious, when he'd been told exactly how young she was which Amanda had understood given her lack of experience but it had been fairly clear he at least liked what he saw.

"Oh trust me, Mr Donaldson, in this getup, there is no way in hell there's any kind of temptation going on, unless it's to burn this monstrosity."

"Sorry, honey." Her father was sitting on a chair, tilting it back, watching the school principal pace the room. Donaldson was biting his lip as he continued to study her with a look of uncertainty.

Bob Moody had offered them the use of a small meeting room within the offices of Knight and Moody. It was sparsely furnished, with three hard chairs which reminded Amanda of the chairs she'd sat on in high school. The small Formica-topped table in the centre of the room had so many scratches in the surface it was hard to see what the original design had been. Amanda had guessed from the little knowledge she had of the style that the table was at least fifty years old. The legs were at least a fairly solid wooden construction, which Amanda assumed was the reason the table had lasted so long.

Her father looked at her with a half-smile, half-sympathetic look. He had invited himself to the meeting and had clearly decided to weigh in on the topic of discussion. He was well aware of her aversion to school uniforms as she had complained almost incessantly about her own during her five years of high school.

"This is the idea of working under cover," he pointed out quietly.

Amanda frowned at him. "I know that Dad. But seriously, it looks like whoever designed this has no sense of style. The skirt is shapeless and as for the material; what do you call it?" She once again plucked at the material which was a mix of bold red, gold and brown in what she assumed was a plaid pattern. "Is it trying to be a tartan or plaid? I don't think it really knows which."

The shirt was just as bad. It might have looked all right on a girl with a less than voluptuous figure but it definitely had not been cut with a fuller figure in mind. The polo shirt just hung on her, almost as if someone had taken a sack and cut holes in it for the neck and sleeves, added a collar and embroidered the school's insignia on it. The huge badge was clearly supposed to be worn with pride, but Amanda imagined the bright gold against the dark red background was the source of some embarrassment for the students. It had been poorly designed, almost as if the designer had fancied him or herself as some kind of reincarnation of Picasso, throwing gold paint at it and hoping for the best.

Amanda looked once again at the principal, who seemed to be doing his best to look affronted and failing miserably. He clearly knew the uniform was not up to scratch, she thought, or else he wouldn't be smirking.

"Why again have you decided to approach a private agency rather than talking to the police?" she asked. The principal appeared to instantly sober with the more serious tone.

Donaldson ran a hand through his hair. It was cut in a style that could be considered 'trendy'. She supposed it was his way of trying to make himself approachable to the students; trying to fit in with the current climate of 'sparing the rod and spoiling the child'. The trouble with that philosophy in her opinion was that the kids emerged from high school with no coping mechanisms. They'd practically had everything handed to them on a silver platter and didn't know the first thing about real competition.

Amanda knew people considered her just as spoiled but the one thing her father had taught her was that disappointment was a part of life. Whenever she had competed in school sports, he'd told her that if she lost, it just meant she had something to aim for in the next competition. It had been meant as encouragement and she took it as such.

Donaldson began relating what had happened to influence his decision to approach Bob Moody. It helped, he told her, that he had known her father for years and it had been his suggestion to go private.

"Surely it's got nothing to do with the kids' rights. I mean, we're talking about illegal drugs not somebody's hairstyle."

She had remembered a case a few years earlier, when she had still been in high school. A teenage boy had been suspended from school for refusing to cut his hair so it conformed with the school's policy. The parents had taken the school board to court saying their son had a right to express his individuality.

"You have a point, Amanda," her father put in, "but the trouble is these are families who have a great deal of political influence."

"So, what you're saying is, they know people in high places. Or rather low, since we are talking about politics."

She glanced at her father, then at Donaldson. Both men were hiding grins behind their hands.

"Crudely put, but yes," Pete replied.

"In other words, these kids could do anything and the parents will just deny it." She huffed. "I mean, come on. Are you seriously telling me you can't even discipline these kids? I mean, I was never that bad in high school. Dad would have throttled me."

"Figuratively speaking, of course," her father returned, smiling at Donaldson.

"Welcome to the new world order," Donaldson replied. "I'm afraid teaching isn't what it was thirty, or even twenty years ago. My hands are tied by the school board."

Amanda rolled her eyes. Of course the board would have much to say about how the students should be disciplined, considering the number of parents who sat on it. It seemed as far as the adults were concerned, their offspring could do no wrong. It would take insurmountable evidence to prove otherwise.

"I've already spoken with a number of board representatives and they each say the same thing. I have to be absolutely certain there is proof of wrongdoing before I involve the authorities."

In other words, Amanda thought, he was between a rock and a hard place. He couldn't get the proof without locker searches but the board had denied permission; afraid of either bad publicity or a lawsuit.

His idea had initially been to have either Moody or Jerry Knight working undercover as a staff member at the school, but after talking with her boss, Donaldson had realised that he needed someone who could actually get close to the students. He needed someone the students would relate to. Someone who was their peer, rather than their teacher. Hence the uniform.

Amanda had thought of nothing else for the entire weekend. She didn't want to say that she doubted her ability to actually do the job, but this was an assignment that even a rookie constable would never have been given.

Then again, her father had also made a very good point when he'd told her that a cop would stick out like a sore thumb. After weeks of training at police college, they would have emerged with a healthy but somewhat mistrustful view of the world.

Amanda at least looked young and naïve - enough that no one would mistake her for a cop, she thought. As long as they didn't try to dig too deep into her 'cover'.

"Amanda, if you don't want to do this …"

She looked at the principal. The man was clearly anxious, worry lines creasing his brow.

"Why is this so important to you?" she asked seriously. "I mean, I know crimes are being committed, but, really, why you, when so many others have most likely put it in the too-hard basket."

Donaldson studied her for a moment, touching his lip.

"I don't mean to …" she began but he shook his head.

"I know what you meant," he said. "And you're right. It is something that has been neglected. But I have to try."

He sat on the desk, leaning slightly forward.

"You know, when I was training to be a teacher, I had so many dreams of being the greatest educator. I always thought my students would love me. They'd learn so much from me." He sighed and shook his head. "These days it's like walking into a battle zone. You never know from one day to the next what you'll strike. The kids are becoming more violent, more belligerent, and you can't discipline them. If it's not the parents or the school board, it's the politicians thinking they're making things better, when really they seem to be making things worse. I've given up trying to understand the constant changes in policy and the way they keep undermining the work of good educators. That doesn't mean, however, that I have given up on the students"

He went on to explain that Fraley High School received much of its funding from the Ministry of Education. It was in a poor area of town with a population of students who came from a variety of backgrounds. Some of them were first generation New Zealanders - their parents having immigrated from the Pacific Islands, or Muslim countries. Some of them, the principal admitted, had committed various crimes, including drug offences. It was inevitable that their children would be caught up in it.

Still others came from reasonably well-off backgrounds and it seemed strange that they would choose to live in a poor end of town. Then again, it was possible that even they couldn't afford the hugely inflated property prices in the central city where the better schools were considered to be.

Donaldson went on. "There is a culture in this school that is terribly wrong and someone has to stand up and say it. Someone has to stop it before an innocent person gets caught in the crossfire. It might as well be me."

Amanda had stared at him through his whole speech, staring at him in wonder. Matt Donaldson could be considered an idealist, but he was pragmatic enough to see the realities of his situation.

"You wanted to make a difference," she said, smiling at him. "You still can."

He smiled back at her, then at her father.

"You were right, Pete."

"About what?" Amanda asked.

"I told him you would understand what he's trying to achieve."

Donaldson's confidence in her seemed to have increased tenfold with that short statement, as did Amanda's own confidence. They ended the meeting on a good note, with Amanda promising to start work at the school in two days.

The principal left the office, appearing happier than when he had first entered.

Amanda grabbed her bundle of clothes, intending to change out of the uniform. Her father stood up.

"Amanda, there's something I need to ..."

"Can it wait a sec, Dad? I need to get out of this

thing."

He nodded. "Fine. How about I take you to lunch? I'll wait here while you change."

Chapter Four

Jim stood just outside the small meeting room, preparing to knock. Just as he lifted his hand, the door opened and Amanda walked out, wearing what Jim could only call the ugliest get-up he'd ever seen.

If that was the uniform, he thought, he'd hate to see the condition of the school. The colours were all wrong and the style was so shapeless a potato sack would have worked just as well. The shirt, if it could be called that, seemed to emphasise all the wrong places. Not that Amanda could be considered fat, but she wasn't skinny either. If he had to admit it, she had a rather nice figure.

Not that he would ever admit to having checked her out.

She stared up at him, craning her neck slightly to compensate for the height difference. Her expression showed surprise.

"What are you doing here?" she asked, her tone

accusing.

"That has got to be the ugliest goddamn get-up I've ever seen," he blurted.

"Nice," she said with a snort. "You wanna get out of my way?"

He stared back at her, eyebrows raised in mock horror. He gestured with his hand, indicating the uniform.

"That's what you have to wear? Good God, I wouldn't wanna be seen dead in something like that."

She looked a little taken aback, her brow furrowed in mild confusion, although she quickly tried to hide it.

"Good thing you don't have to then," she retorted rudely. "Excuse me."

His boss appeared in the doorway as the blonde strode off holding a bundle of clothing.

"Jim. Thanks for coming."

"Sure. No problem. Uh, she does know, right?"

Pete bit his lip and ran a hand through his greying blond hair. "Yeah, I haven't exactly broken the news to her."

Oh great, Jim thought.

The detective sergeant waved him into the meeting room. It was small, reminding him of an interrogation room at the police station. Even the furniture appeared to give off that impression.

It seemed appropriate, given what his boss had told him about the man Amanda was working for. Jim hadn't known Bob Moody, since the former police officer had resigned from his job long before Jim had moved north, but everything about the office reflected a man who had worked in law enforcement. The meeting rooms were sparsely furnished, with practicality rather than comfort in mind.

"We just got through a meeting with Matt Donaldson," Pete was explaining.

Jim looked at him questioningly.

"The school principal," his boss added.

"Oh. How'd it go?"

"I've known Matt for a few years. Actually, don't tell Amanda this, but Matt was a bit of a hellraiser when I first met him. He was Amanda's age and got himself into a bit of trouble." He laughed and shook his head. Jim was curious to know what the man had done, but his boss didn't elaborate as he continued. "Thought he could outsmart us cops. Instead, he got a wake-up call. Judge told him he needed to smarten up before he ended up in prison."

His boss went on to explain that the youth had been given one chance to prove himself. He'd been sentenced to community service and had chosen to work at a youth centre. It had opened his eyes and inspired him to become a teacher.

The door opened and Amanda walked in, wearing a black pencil skirt and black and white striped blouse in what appeared to be satin. Much better, Jim thought.

She sighed as she put down the bundle she had

been carrying and glared at him before turning back to her father.

"So? What's he doing here?"

"That's what I was going to tell you," the detective sergeant replied. "I asked Jim to liaise with you. In case anything goes sour."

She stared at her father, looking incredulous.

"You don't trust me?"

"It's not that, honey. I just want you to be safe."

She looked even more annoyed at that. Jim could understand her attitude. It did imply a little that his boss couldn't trust his own daughter's abilities, but he could also see it from his boss' point of view. From what he'd gleaned so far, this wasn't just a simple matter of kids smoking marijuana or taking party drugs. Donaldson thought some of his students were getting into serious Class A drugs, although he had no proof. Jim hoped Amanda's father had made it clear to her she was only there to get evidence that could be followed up by police and not try to perform any heroics herself.

"I can't believe you Dad! You seriously want me to work with him? He's a troglodyte!"

Jim huffed loudly at the word, glowering at her. She smirked at him.

"I'm sorry! Would you prefer another term? How about Neanderthal?" He choked. "Hmm, no, I'm guessing words of more than two syllables would be too much for you to handle. How about caveman?"

Okay, he thought. I don't have to take this from

some jumped-up little princess who thinks she's better than me simply because her father's my boss. "Just who the hell do you think you are, little girl?" he said silently, narrowing his eyes at her.

"Bitch!" The word came out before he could even think to filter his language. He shot a glance at his boss, who was just watching them, his gaze moving back and forth as if he was an umpire at a tennis match. He seemed faintly amused as they began to exchange insults.

"Jerk!"

"Brat!" His glare was almost glacial. At least, he hoped so. "You know I might have to work with you, princess, but I sure as hell don't have to like you."

Her glare was the opposite, as if she wished she could set him on fire.

"I suppose you think you're God's gift!" she growled.

More insults followed. Jim finally turned to look at his boss.

"She can't do it," he said. "She's too immature!"

Amanda huffed loudly in protest, calling him a jerk.

"That the best you can come up with?" he scoffed.

Peter held up his hands as if he was a referee at a fight, forcing them apart before the bickering could devolve any further.

"All right. Cut it out! The pair of you. Before I start knocking some heads together." He glared at

Jim. "Act your age. And stop antagonising her!" He then turned his glare on his daughter. "And you ... try to act like a lady, if that's even possible!"

Amanda spluttered, trying to act as if none of this was her fault. Her father continued to glare at her.

"I mean it, Amanda. This is not going to be a walk-in-the-park. Most girls your age wouldn't even dream of getting an opportunity like this and I'm not going to let you blow it because you can't work with the man I've asked to keep you safe. So you do as you're told and stop whining!"

Fuming, Amanda glared at Jim, who glared back, arms folded. Sighing, Pete walked out, leaving them to it. Jim looked at her. Amanda stood in the middle of the room, a stubborn look on her face. He huffed and started to follow his boss out the door, then paused to look back at her.

"By the way, a troglodyte is a cave dweller, not a caveman. There's a difference. If you're going to insult someone, get your definitions right."

Amanda snorted. "Potayto potahto."

He chose to ignore that, continuing to follow his boss. Amanda joined them shortly after, her heels clicking on the hardwood floor as she hurried to catch up with them. Pete paused at the exit and looked at him.

"Coming to lunch with us, Jim?"

From the way the blonde was glaring at him, Jim got the feeling he wouldn't be welcome.

"Uh, no. Figured I'd head back to the office. Got that robbery case I'm working on."

"Good," Amanda said. It was clearly supposed to have only been loud enough for him to hear, but from the way his boss glared at the girl, he'd heard it anyway.

He returned to work, intending to focus on the case, but couldn't help thinking about the girl. If she could just cool it with the obnoxious attitude, she might actually be good at her job. From the way she spoke, she was clearly articulate and intelligent, even if she only used it to insult him. She was obviously a young woman who was used to having things her own way.

He would never admit it in a million years; not to her at least, but he liked her. Amanda had what his parents liked to call 'spunk'. She was definitely spirited, he thought.

That didn't mean, however, that he was going to like working with her. As much as he liked his boss the girl was going to be a pain in the ass and that was an understatement!

He was packing up his desk for the day when Pete stopped by. "Jim."

He looked up at the older man. "Yeah, boss?"

"Look," Pete said, running a hand through his hair and tousling it. "I know my daughter can be a pain in the proverbial. Sometimes I think she's too smart for her own good."

Jim nodded, picking up his bottle of water, not wanting to comment in case he said something he shouldn't.

"I do appreciate you taking this job on," the

detective-sergeant continued. "However, this little mutual antagonism you've got with her isn't helping."

"Boss, I get that, but she started it."

His boss looked at him with an expression akin to asking: 'Are you twelve?'

"She called me a troglodyte," he said defensively.

"You don't have to retaliate!" Pete returned. "Just … try to get along with her. I know how impossible she can be, but she's a good girl, really."

Yeah, maybe if she was taken down a peg or two, Jim thought. His boss started to walk away, then stopped and looked at him. Jim tipped his bottle up to take a long, refreshing drink of cold water.

"You know, all that bickering … well, in my day, we would have called that foreplay."

Jim choked on his water, spraying it all over the papers on his desk. Pete laughed and walked away.

Jim flopped down in his chair. Foreplay? Oh dear god, I hope not, he thought.

Chapter Five

The teacher didn't bother to introduce her to the class when Amanda entered the classroom on her first day. The kids stared at her, some with curious expressions while others just smirked, then proceeded to ignore her.

There was only one empty desk, at the back of the classroom. Amanda made her way up the row, her gaze firmly facing forward, pretending she was nervous. A boy aged about seventeen sitting at the desk beside the empty one looked at her, before quickly looking away.

Donaldson hadn't given her any suggestions for a cover story, so she had spent a few days making up something. Despite her reservations about being forced to liaise with the detective constable, her father had told her any issues relating to the job should be discussed with Jim Andersen, rather than him. Reluctantly, Amanda had taken her idea for a cover to the detective. He'd agreed, ensuring Donaldson also understood what it entailed.

Jim had given her the impression that he hadn't liked her very much. She knew she hadn't exactly made the best first impression, although she had rather enjoyed bickering with him. At least the man gave as good as he got, she thought.

"Are we boring you, Miss Carter?"

For a moment Amanda was confused, until she remembered she had told Donaldson not to use her real name, in case someone made the connection to her father. She stared with a perplexed frown at the teacher, who glared back with a look of impatience.

"Miss?" she said, trying to make her tone sound put-out that she had been called on already. While the idea had been for her to act as if school was the last place she wanted to be, she hadn't been prepared to be the centre of attention within an hour of being inside the school. Or to be caught daydreaming. Get with the program, she told herself silently.

"What's the answer to the problem on the board?" the teacher asked, huffing in annoyance. Amanda could feel herself growing hot, conscious of the smirks from the rest of the students.

She stared at the mathematical formula on the board. Maths had been one of her stronger subjects at school. She could have easily solved the problem but she wasn't here for that. If she wanted the kids in the class to relate to her, she couldn't be seen to be smarter than they were.

"Um, I don't know," she said.

The teacher rolled her eyes before turning to another student and asking the same question. The woman had probably only got her degree a couple of years ago. She was clearly not much older than her students. Less than ten years anyway, Amanda thought. Still, she was too young to be as apathetic as she looked.

Amanda sneaked a glance at the teacher, then dug in her pocket to pull out a wrapped stick of gum. She slowly unwrapped it, pretending to be watching the teacher, while watching the boy next to her out of the corner of her eye. He seemed riveted as she put the gum in her mouth, his attention fully on her.

When she had met with Donaldson again late the week before, he'd given her some files to study on students known to be the ringleaders. He hadn't known with any certainty that they were the ones behind the drug problems plaguing the school, but it was a place to start.

By the time her first day was over, Amanda had heard enough to know other students were talking about her. Most had the impression she was little more than a 'dumb blonde' but there had been at least a couple who wondered if there was more to it.

She joined the throng of students doing their level best to leave school grounds as quickly as humanly possible, pretending to be just as eager. Donaldson was on the gate, watching the teenagers passing by. He spotted her and raised an eyebrow but she shook her head. Meeting on school grounds was not a good idea.

Reporting back to the office, Amanda changed out of the uniform into something more comfortable and sat down at the desk she'd been assigned to write up her daily report on the laptop. It was an older model and thus a little slow, but was sufficiently adequate for writing. Anything else would need a more powerful processor, she thought.

She looked up when she heard a knock on the door. Bob Moody frowned at her.

"How did the first day go?"

She shrugged. "Fine. I'm not exactly expecting to solve the case in one day."

"Donaldson phoned. He wanted to know if you'd made any progress."

"If I had something to report, he'd know," she told her boss, trying to keep her tone even, although it still came out 'snippy'. He raised an eyebrow at her.

"It's just ... he's expecting a lot if he wants me to find it all out in one day," she explained. "I mean, the idea of working undercover is ... well, you'd know. You can't exactly walk in there and start asking questions. The kids will get suspicious."

He nodded. "Of course. But I hope you have some idea of where to go with this. You know the pressure he's under."

Donaldson had told her the board had hired him hoping he would be able to work miracles in the school. She again had that feeling that Donaldson was between a rock and a hard place. The board members seemed to be acting like ostriches with their heads in the sand, pretending the problems weren't as bad as the principal feared, yet expected the school to raise its level of performance in qualifying examinations.

Amanda had done enough research on the school to know that it was one of the lowest in the country when it came to grades on the National Certificate. What Donaldson hadn't told her, but her research had uncovered, was that the school was in serious danger of being closed by the Ministry of Education. The rumours of criminal activity as well as the poorly performing students had the government reaching for the proverbial chequebook, if only to keep it closed.

It went without saying that a lot of students would miss out if the school was forced to close. Given the government's rules on zoning, some of the population would be considered 'out of zone' of other schools.

Amanda sighed. She certainly had her work cut out for her.

Chapter Six

Jim had spent the better part of a week doing research on Fraley High School, wanting to give himself a better idea of what to expect. Out of five hundred students, more than half had already appeared in court for juvenile offences. Some of them included drugs - either possession or selling.

What he'd read had only served to make him more uneasy about Amanda going in undercover. She was untrained and as far as he was concerned, way out of her depth.

Not that he was actually concerned about her or anything, he thought. She clearly thought she could handle it and wasn't about to listen to him, or anyone else for that matter.

Since he was supposed to be liaising with her, he knew he would have to meet with her at some point. The past few days an investigation on an armed robbery had kept him from working on the school case, but a lull in proceedings reminded him he needed to catch up with Amanda.

Deciding to bite the bullet, Jim called her and arranged to meet with her at a downtown café/bar. Vigueur Café was close to the waterfront, but not so close that it was crowded on a Tuesday evening. He could see a few families together either already eating or getting ready to order a meal. The café was a fairly popular place as it was considered family friendly.

Amanda walked in just as Jim was shown to a table by the hostess of the night. He nodded at her, remaining standing as she approached him. She paused mid-stride, glancing around before reaching their table.

"Hello," he said, waiting as she dumped her bag on the table and sat down. "How are you doing?" Never let it be said that his parents hadn't taught him manners.

Amanda said nothing, not even a 'hello' in return. He frowned. Her father would have taught her better than that.

"So, how's it going?" he said, trying again to at least engage in polite conversation. She was clearly having none of it.

"How's what going?" she replied, frowning at him.

He suppressed the urge to roll his eyes. With some women, they could be so literal. He guessed Amanda was one of them.

"It's called small talk."

She scowled. "Look, you called me to meet you here, obviously to talk about what I have or haven't

found out, so why don't we cut the chatter and just
…"

She broke off as the waitress came to take their orders. Amanda hadn't even picked up her menu.

"I haven't even looked at the menu yet," she snapped. The young woman, a blonde about Amanda's age, looked taken aback.

"Fine," she said, pressing her lips together in a hard line. "I'll give you a few more minutes."

Jim glared at Amanda. "That was rude."

"So? She barely gave me a chance to sit down."

"Lighten up, Amanda. Ever think that maybe she's just trying to be efficient?"

"She's a waitress," she replied snottily, as if a job as a waitress was beneath her. Jim figured she was just in a bad mood, since she'd been belligerent since walking into the bar, but that was just bad manners.

He huffed. Okay, he thought. Who put the stick up your butt?

"Why don't you grow up and try to remember that the world does not revolve around you?" he shot back.

Amanda looked mutinous, but picked up her menu, her eyes scanning the page as she perused her choices. Jim smiled as the waitress returned.

"Sorry about my 'friend'," he told her, emphasising the word to show he meant exactly the opposite. "She's one of those girls who likes to think she's low maintenance but she's really high maintenance."

He snickered, realising from the way Amanda stiffened that she knew what he meant. The waitress grinned back at him, appearing unfazed.

"Don't worry about it," she replied. "You get used to the sucky ones in this job."

He continued chatting to her as she wrote down his order, complimenting her on her easy manner.

Amanda interrupted them, giving her own order. Jim ignored her and deliberately turned in his seat to watch the waitress walking away. The sudden snapping of fingers in his face had him turning back to face his dining companion.

"Hello? Remember me? The girl you invited here? It's rude to flirt with someone else in front of someone you invited."

He glowered at her. "Let's get one thing straight, Miss Stick-Up-My-Butt. This is not a date. This is a business meeting. And trust me, I don't like this any more than you do, so get off your high horse."

He leaned forward, deciding to change the subject.

"So, what have you found out so far."

"Nothing. As in zip, zilch, nada."

"Nothing at all?" he asked, surprised.

"It's only been two days! What did you expect?"

"I've been studying the records for some of these kids and we're not just dealing with minor misdemeanours. We're talking serious crime."

"I'm not stupid. I have done my own research you know."

He sighed. "Well, you sure as hell don't have to

worry about not fitting in at that school. Two days and you're already acting like them."

She scowled at him.

"What is that supposed to mean?"

"I mean, you're acting like a teenager."

"Uh, newsflash, bub, I am a teenager. And I will be for another two months."

"God help us all," he retorted.

Their food was brought to the table, but the meal was an exercise in torture. Jim had no complaints about the food, but he couldn't say the same about his dinner companion. She couldn't have been more disagreeable if she tried.

If she could just get rid of that huge chip on her shoulder, he thought, she might actually be someone worth getting to know.

He had no idea if it was just him that set her off, or something else. The more he tried not to antagonise her, the more she appeared to dig her heels in. Which didn't help him stick to his resolve to at least try to get along with her, if only for his boss' sake.

He was working at his desk the next day when his boss appeared beside him.

"Got a minute?"

He nodded, getting up to follow Pete to his office. The sergeant nodded at him.

"Close the door."

Jim waited as his boss sat down behind his desk, looking contemplative.

"So, Amanda called me last night."

"Let me guess. Complaining about me."

Pete grinned, relaxing. "Pretty much. Damn, that kid will talk your ear off if you let her."

That was hardly the experience he had the night before. When Amanda wasn't being argumentative, she would sit and sulk, looking more and more like a petulant child.

Which didn't match with the stories he'd heard about her from around the station. He had heard Kerry, the area commander's secretary, tell a few stories about her 'best friend'. Kerry had apparently known Amanda for quite a few years, despite being a few years older than her. It seemed Amanda was a fairly regular visitor to the station. Amanda was considered a bright, gregarious young woman who was usually very friendly to his co-workers.

So what was it about him that had her acting the opposite?

Then again, her behaviour the night before seemed to be different again from the way she'd behaved toward him the week before. Then it had almost seemed as if she enjoyed exchanging barbs with him. Last night, she had been, for want of a better word, a bitch.

"Maybe I'm seeing a different side to her."

"Yeah, I get that." The boss sighed. "Look, Jim, I know she can be difficult and spoiled. That's probably my fault. When you're a single parent … well, I guess you spend half your time trying to be both Mum and Dad. I'm afraid I wasn't very good at it. Amanda hasn't been around a lot of men.

Again, my fault."

Jim shrugged and sat down. He knew how hard it had been for his own father before he'd married Lesleigh, his stepmother. Jim's mother had died not long after he was born and Eric had spent a few years trying to cope with his young son on his own. "You were just trying to be protective."

"My daughter accuses me of being over-protective, and maybe she's right. Maybe I was asking too much to expect her to work with you. I guess in her mind it sounds like I don't trust her. In her words: 'I don't need a babysitter!'"

"I would have to disagree, boss. Especially after what I've been seeing. These kids aren't just your normal, run-of-the-mill troublemakers. There are serious crimes being committed."

The sergeant looked at him with a sardonic lift of his eyebrow.

"Try telling my daughter that. She's so goddamn stubborn. I don't know where she gets it from."

Jim decided it was safer not to comment on that.

Chapter Seven

Amanda glared at her reflection in the mirror. She'd been at this school four days so far hadn't learnt a damn thing. The principal was counting on her to find out who was dealing and help him clear up the drug problem.

Half of the problem was that she had been too overconfident in thinking this would just be an easy case. Some of the blame could be directed at a certain detective constable. Well, maybe not blame exactly. Still, if the man hadn't got her back up and looked at her like an idiot, she wouldn't have felt the need to prove him wrong.

The trouble was she was proving him right. She had no idea what she was supposed to do. There was no guideline, no instruction book, no YouTube how-to guide on how to get in with the 'in crowd', so to speak.

She remembered once in English class the teacher had assigned them research on idioms and their origins. She'd been given one: 'hoist with one's own petard'. Well, she'd been hoisted all right.

She sighed as she stared once more at her reflection.

"You, my friend, are a first rate idiot."

It wasn't the first time she'd got herself into trouble over a guy. She had always hated being pigeonholed, or maybe stereotyped was the better word, she thought. Even her high school friends had treated her as if she was a dumb blonde and of course she'd had to prove them wrong. She'd considered it a challenge to show them just how dumb she wasn't.

There had been a guy in her Year Twelve biology class who had assumed the same as everyone else. He'd teased her for her looks, telling all his mates she couldn't possibly be smart enough or athletic enough to climb on to the roof of the school gym without getting caught, or without fear of breaking a nail.

Annoyed at the implication that she was that shallow, Amanda had taken the challenge. She'd just managed to get to the roof when the principal had caught her. That had resulted in a visit and a severe dressing down from her father, who had been not only angry but also worried. She could have broken her neck; or worse.

Despite the disastrous end to her little adventure, she'd managed to earn the grudging respect of not only her peers, but the classmate she had had a crush on all year. While she hadn't done it just to impress him, she had been more than happy when he'd begun talking to her and had finally asked her out.

Amanda thought she had learnt her lesson, especially after the guy had turned out to be a complete jerk. Now here she was doing it again. Only this wasn't just a stunt. This was much, much worse.

"Idiot," she told herself, shaking her head at her reflection. "Bloody idiot."

"You know, talking to yourself is never a good sign," a voice said, sounding amused.

Amanda turned her head and looked at the pretty brunette, realising she had come out of the cubicle which had been closed when she'd first entered the bathroom.

"Yeah?" she said.

The girl grinned and nodded.

"Yeah. I think you're okay though. I mean it's not like you're, you know, talking to people who aren't there. Not unless the bathroom is haunted."

She smiled ruefully, then washed her hands.

"I guess."

"So, uh, you're new, huh?" The brunette laughed. "God, how lame is that? Of course you're new. I mean, it's not like you were here last week. Okay, I'm done being an idiot. See, you've got me doing it too." She laughed again. "I'm babbling."

"No worries," Amanda replied.

"I'm Lori. You're … Amanda, right?"

She nodded. "Yeah."

"So where you coming from?" Lori asked,

leaning over the sink to wave her hand under the automatic soap dispenser before washing her hands.

"Class."

Lori tittered. "Oh sure, be literal. I mean, what school did you go to before?"

"St Anne's. Down south."

Jim had told her he'd talked to an old friend who had been able to set it all up for them. She had been only too happy to provide the back-up information in case anyone ever asked about Amanda.

"How come you're here?" Lori asked.

Amanda quickly averted her gaze, letting her body language speak for itself. She'd never been particularly good at acting, but she figured breaking eye contact would be enough to let her avoid completely lying.

"My parents figured I needed a fresh start," she said. "I'm boarding in the city."

They left the bathroom together and began walking down the hallway. Lori stopped at a door leading to the quad.

"My friends are just out there," she said. "Why don't you join us?"

Amanda was torn between heading to the office to see what she could find out about Lori and joining the younger girl. She hesitated, then began following the brunette.

The 'friends' included the youth she'd sat next to in the maths class on her first day. He looked her over and smirked.

"Where'd you dig this one up, Lori?" he said.

The brunette rolled her eyes.

"Shut up, moron." She turned back to Amanda. "That one's Kyle. Ignore him. He's an ass."

"Speak for yourself," Kyle replied.

Amanda studied Kyle. Despite the school uniform and the short hair style, he somehow managed to look scruffier than most. There was nothing she could really pin down as the cause. His uniform was no worse than any others, although his hair looked as if it hadn't been combed in days. His face was covered in acne, although again that was fairly typical of all the boys in the group.

He seemed to have a way of sitting as if he didn't give a damn about anything. As she stood beside Lori he leaned over and she caught a whiff of stale cigarette smoke. His whole body reeked of a sickly sweet odour that made her want to retch.

Lori introduced the others, but Amanda didn't catch all of their names. A tall boy from another of her classes smirked at her.

"Didn't I see you the other night with some old guy?"

She frowned at him, feigning ignorance, inwardly smirking at the thought that Jim was being described as an 'old guy' by an eighteen-year-old boy, in spite of the fact that he was less than ten years older than her.

"In Vigueur, down by the waterfront. He your brother or something?"

She shrugged. Jim was probably more than

pissed off with her for the way she had acted the other night, but when she had recognised a couple of teenagers from the school, she had decided to act as if having dinner with Jim was the last thing she wanted to be doing. She had been worried they might have recognised him as a cop, although since he had only transferred a couple of months earlier the chances he was known in the area were fairly slim.

That didn't mean, however, that she was at all happy with the way he was treating her. She knew he thought she was in over her head. She wasn't about to give him the satisfaction of knowing he was right.

"He looked kinda pissed," the boy continued.

"Yeah, he tries to make out like he's looking out for me," she said, not completely untruthfully. "You know, stuck in the big bad city and everything. I can't stand him."

"So where did you come from?"

"St Anne's," she said.

"St Anne's where?" Kyle asked, narrowing his eyes at her.

"Down south," she said evasively, which only made him appear more suspicious.

"Why'd you move here?" Lori asked.

"Um, family stuff," she replied, quickly trying to change the subject.

Amanda had read enough to know these kids were fairly smart and would swiftly grow suspicious enough to do some checking. She hoped she had managed to make up enough information that her cover would survive that kind of scrutiny, particularly if one of the teens she was investigating had any kind of hacking skills.

From the intensity of the stare from the youth, she wondered if she had done enough to survive such scrutiny. God only knew what the kid was thinking.

She tried to pretend it didn't bother her, but some of the things Jim had been saying had actually got to her. Not that his opinions mattered, she thought. She might be nineteen, but she was still an adult and his view of her as an immature child who was incapable of carrying out such a task as this investigation still rankled.

She had considered calling him to apologise for the other night, but after her father had reported the conversation between him and the detective, she decided he could go to hell.

Amanda continued sitting with the other kids, long after the lunch period had ended, listening in on the conversation. A few of them had already made plans to meet up at a local bar the next evening. One where the bouncers apparently didn't check i.d.s that closely. She noticed no such invitation was extended to her, but she decided she would go anyway. If anything was going to lead her to whoever was dealing drugs in the school, this had to be it.

"Besides," she said to herself. "What other leads do you have?"

Much to her annoyance, as she was getting ready to go out the next night, Jim showed up at her flat. Her flatmate Penny looked at her questioningly as she went out to the living room to talk to him.

"What do you want?" she asked tersely.

"You didn't call to report in," he said.

She stared at him. "Was I supposed to? Last I checked, I was autonomous in this."

He raised an eyebrow and smirked at her.

"Autonomous? That's a big word for you."

Oh, she so wanted to smack that smirk right off his face. On a deeper level, she figured she deserved to be mocked, considering the way she had insulted him the week before. It didn't mean, however, that she was just going to let him get away with it.

"Yeah? At least I have a brain. You're more the brawn in this relationship."

He snickered. "Relationship? Let's get one thing straight, Princess. The only relationship between you and I," he added, gesturing with his hand back and forth between them, "is you being a pain in my ass."

"Stop calling me Princess," she responded angrily. Even the knowledge that he was only doing it to get a rise out of her didn't stop her from getting annoyed.

"Not in a million years!" he replied, clearly enjoying himself.

"You're a jerk."

"Go ahead, stamp your feet, have your little tantrum. But next time, when I leave a message for you to call me, I expect you to do just that."

Amanda hadn't even looked at her phone and wasn't even aware he had left a message. Not that she was going to tell him that.

"I was ignoring you," she lied.

"Don't make me call your dad," he said. "Your father asked me to keep an eye on things. How am I going to do that if you're ignoring my calls?"

"Gee, I don't know. Learn to become a psychic? I didn't want to work with you in the first place!"

"Feeling's mutual!" he hissed. He turned to leave, then hesitated. "By the way, my friend called and told me someone hacked into the file."

She nodded. She'd expected that. After all, these kids weren't exactly stupid.

"I figured they would," she said.

"I hope to God you know what you're doing, Amanda. These kids aren't playing games."

"I know that," she replied. "I'm not stupid."

He studied her for a long moment, then nodded before turning and walking away. Amanda stood in the doorway, biting her lip. She knew she should have just been honest with him, but something about him just always seemed to get her back up.

Chapter Eight

Jim had got off duty hours ago, but he decided to spend the night working on his laptop at the desk in his bedroom. There was something about this whole case that bothered him. It wasn't just the fact that Amanda was going in to what was starting to look like a very bad situation. It was that these kids seemed far too smart for their own good.

Amanda was an intelligent girl; he would give her that. Despite her accusations, he didn't think she was at all stupid. A little arrogant, or perhaps overconfident was more the word. She was, after all, only nineteen. Pete was right. At that age, she was still thinking like a teenager rather than an adult, thus thinking she knew everything.

Maybe at twenty-six, he was still fairly young, considering, but at least he had some experience behind him. Two years serving in the army had given him some toughness and some life skills that had helped him in his application for police training. He just didn't see that kind of toughness in Amanda.

Granted, part of the problem was her father had tried to protect her from the worst of his job. He could understand why. Given the fact he'd raised her alone since she was eight, it was inevitable that some things in her personal growth would have been lacking. Having seen as much as he had in his six years as a cop himself, Jim could also understand his boss' reluctance to expose his only child to it through her formative years. What that meant was that as much as she thought she knew about the world, experiencing it was another matter.

As much as she clearly didn't want to admit it, Jim thought even Amanda had realised she was in way over her head. The question was, what did he do about it? He couldn't exactly go to his boss. They'd already talked about the problem and Pete seemed to think his daughter could handle herself.

Talking to Amanda wasn't going to work either. It would just go in one ear and out the other. She was a stubborn young woman; that much was obvious.

"Hey, you coming out to join us?"

Jim looked up and stared at his fair-haired flatmate. Craig was a decent enough guy. He worked in real estate, while his partner, Susan, was an accounts administrator for a local wholesaler.

The couple were once again having a party. Jim had been so deep in thought that he hadn't heard people arriving.

"Uh, I really should …" he said, gesturing to the laptop.

"Come on," Craig said. "You hardly spend any time with us as it is. It's Friday night. You're not on duty this weekend."

He sighed and bit his lip. He didn't want his flatmates thinking he was unsociable, but he really thought he should focus on what he was doing.

Then again, maybe his flatmates could help provide some insight into the dilemma.

Closing down the lid of the laptop, Jim got up to join Craig. He followed him down the hallway and out through the sliding doors to the patio.

"Guess who decided to join us," he said.

Susan smiled. "Hey flattie," she greeted him warmly.

"Hey."

Craig thrust a bottle of beer in his hand.

"So, what's been happening at work?" Susan asked.

"Uh, well, the usual, I guess. My boss asked me to liaise with this private investigator on a case. I'm just not sure it should be handled by this investigator."

Susan's forehead creased in a frown. She tossed her dark honey coloured hair.

"Why?" she asked. "Is it dangerous?"

"Potentially, yeah. The thing is, the investigator … She's young. This is her first job. The only reason she got it is because, well, I think because of her dad." He explained the situation as best he could without giving too much of it away. Susan's green eyes sparkled as she smiled.

"Well, if you want my two cents, I think you like this girl."

"No," he scoffed.

"Suze has a point," Craig replied, his arm around his girlfriend's shoulders. He had a bottle of beer in his other hand. "The way you talk about her it's like there's some kind of spark between you."

"I do not like her like that," Jim told his flatmate.

"Yet you're clearly worried about her," Angela, a woman who worked with Susan told him. "And not in a … 'I don't think she can handle this' way."

He tried to protest, but all the others who had been listening to his story nodded their agreement.

"So, what do I do?" he asked, shrugging in resignation. They obviously thought they knew how he felt better than he did.

Craig clapped him on the shoulder.

"Afraid you're not going to win with this girl. Sounds to me like she's the type of girl who once she's made up her mind, nothing you say or do is going to change it."

He groaned quietly.

"Personally I think you've got the proverbial tiger by the tail," Angela put in. "If you want my advice, I'd say leave her be. She's not going to welcome your opinion, no matter what you say. The best you can do is continue to keep an eye on things and only when things look like they're getting out of hand, then you step in."

As good as the advice was, he knew there was far more to it than that. If things did indeed get out of hand, it wouldn't just cost Amanda her job. It could cost her life and that was something Jim just wasn't willing to allow.

Okay, he thought, maybe there is more than just concern for a co-worker, if she could be called that. His flatmates and their friends were right. Despite the apparent hostility between them, he liked the girl. Sure, she was young, and had a lot of maturing to do, but that wasn't necessarily a bad thing.

The question was, what did he do about it?

He ran a hand over his dark hair, sighing. The definition of insanity, he thought, was doing the same thing over and over and expecting a different result. It didn't matter how much he went over and over it in his head. He wasn't going to get the answer he was looking for.

A hand clapped on his shoulder and he looked around to see a man in his forties, his blue eyes twinkling merrily.

"Trust me, mate, it never gets any easier the older you get. Been married twenty years and my wife still doesn't think I understand women."

Angela snorted.

"Hey, it's not any better for us women, you know. Sometimes I think it's worse when your significant other is the same sex. Lisa practically thinks I should be able to read her mind."

"Talking about me?" A woman with reddish-brown hair cut in a boyish short style approached them, wrapping her arm around Angela's waist. Jim quickly noticed the gold band on her right ring finger.

Angela smiled; a slightly guilty sort of smile which she was clearly using to try to convince her partner they hadn't been talking about her.

"No, sweetie, of course not."

"Yeah, right," Lisa replied with a snort. "Contrary to popular belief, I do not always think you should be able to read my mind. I, on the other hand, can read you like a book, especially when you get that guilty look on your face."

Angela flushed. "Uh, babe, you know I was just …"

"Yeah, I know what you were just," her partner responded, guiding her away from the men.

Jim couldn't help chuckling as the two women began bickering. Sounded a little like him and Amanda, he thought.

"Oh, god, what a disaster that would be," he said to himself.

Chapter Nine

Amanda had been sitting in the corner of the bar watching the main door for about an hour when the group of students showed up. She remained where she was, pretending she didn't care if they spotted her or not.

With the exception of Lori, who was in a couple of the same classes, they'd basically ignored her for most of the day.

She fiddled with the straw in her drink. She had wanted to keep her head clear so she had ordered orange juice. Not that it helped, since all she could think about was the pressure she was under.

If it wasn't bad enough that Jim had taken her to task for not keeping her end of the deal, Donaldson had also called asking for an update. She knew how much stress he was under. Despite the principal's efforts to keep the problems at the school under wraps, the Ministry had somehow found out and was sending someone next month to assess the school. The man's job was on the line.

She felt bad for the guy but there was only so much she could do. She hoped she had laid down enough groundwork so she could continue fooling the students into giving themselves away, but she knew it wasn't going to be that simple, considering her inexperience

"Amanda? Hey!"

She looked up and smiled at Lori.

"Hey Lori."

"How did you get in? I thought you weren't eighteen yet?"

She shrugged. Since the bar's staff didn't seem to care about the laws restricting entry to those under eighteen, she hadn't even had to worry about pretending to have a fake i.d. They hadn't even bothered to card her.

"Yo Lori, what's she doing here?"

Amanda scowled at Kyle. There was something about the guy she just didn't like and it was fairly clear the feeling was mutual. Tonight he looked even more unkempt than usual.

"What are you looking at?" Kyle asked, sounding accusing.

"Not you," she replied smartly.

"Who said you could come hang out here?" he asked, reaching for her glass. Amanda frowned at him and pulled it away.

"You're not the boss of me," she told him. "I can hang out where I want."

"Yeah?" Another boy spoke up. "Who said?"

"Yeah, this is our place. No newbies allowed."

"Territorial much?" she asked. "You don't own the place so don't tell me what to do!"

She got up and took her glass with her. Lori followed her to the bar, leaning on it as Amanda ordered another drink, this time a vodka and orange, hoping Lori would be fooled into thinking she had been drinking that all this time. As much as she liked the pretty brunette, she knew she had to be cautious.

"Ignore those guys," Lori told her. "They're just jerks."

Amanda shrugged and glanced back to the corner where they were still standing.

"Yeah, I know they are." She frowned at the girl. "Why do you hang out with them, anyway?"

"Jake's, well, he's sort of my cousin. I mean, he is, but like second cousin. My Gran's his auntie."

Lori pointed out a boy with blond hair the colour of straw. It even looked the same texture.

Jake seemed to be a fairly decent guy. He'd been friendly toward her. Considering the hostility coming from Kyle, even just a modicum of pretence at civility was an improvement. Despite his more approachable manner, she had the feeling he was just as suspicious of her as Kyle. While she'd never studied psychology, even she understood that it was the quiet ones who needed watching the most.

She took her drink back to her table, only to find the boys had taken over. Kyle was sitting on the stool she had just vacated.

"You're in my seat," she said crossly.

"Didn't see your name on it," he returned with a smirk.

Lori sighed beside her.

"Way to make a girl feel wanted," she said. "Like I said, jerks."

Kyle glared at Lori, but shifted. "How 'bout we share?" he suggested with a sly grin.

Amanda wrinkled her nose.

"How about no?" she said. "I wouldn't touch you with a ten-foot pole!"

The greasy-haired youth snorted.

"Don't flatter yourself Princess!"

Another one who liked to get up her back, she thought. She had never let her father get away with calling her Princess and she wasn't about to let some jumped-up troll call her one either.

There was no way to win this one and it wasn't going to help her case any either, she thought. She was supposed to be getting close to the students, not alienating them.

Amanda stayed by the table and chatted with Lori. The two boys soon grew weary of the 'girl talk' and got up to move. She watched them, noting they didn't head for the exit; nor did they head for the bathroom.

"I should follow them," she said to herself, starting to move from the table. Lori caught her arm.

"Where are you going?"

She looked at the younger girl, then grimaced and shifted as if she had an urgent need to be somewhere else.

"I gotta go to the bathroom," she told Lori. "Watch my drink?"

"Sure."

"Be right back."

She made her way through the crowd toward the bathroom, glancing back to make sure Lori wasn't watching before changing direction. The two boys had also disappeared in the throng of people. The small delay had cost her.

Amanda continued looking around for them and spotted a sign for the emergency exit near the kitchen. Fortunately, the kitchen wasn't busy this time of night as the bar stopped serving from their small menu after ten. Which meant there was no one to stop people using that exit.

Amanda once more glanced toward the table where Lori was waiting before carefully opening the door. It led to what seemed to be a storeroom beyond which was another door leading to an outer exit which was slightly ajar.

Hearing voices, Amanda moved to the second door and looked out the narrow window. There was just enough light from the street light at the end of the alley that she could see a few people gathered by the exit. One of them she recognised as one of the younger bartenders.

She remained in the darkness of the storeroom, straining to hear the conversation. The people were gathered a short distance away but just far enough that she couldn't understand what was being said.

Amanda debated whether she should open the door further to hear what was going on. She had just put her hand on the handle when she spotted Kyle and Jake. They had their heads bent and appeared to be exchanging something. She could see Kyle had a lit cigarette in his hand. At least it looked like a cigarette.

She caught a whiff of a very strong odour that smelled almost like burnt rubber drifting in through the doorway. It reminded her a little of coffee beans that had been roasted until they were burnt. Marijuana, she thought.

One of the people in the alley began moving toward the door. Amanda quickly stepped back before turning to leave the storeroom. She returned to the bar and made her way back to Lori.

"What took so long?" Lori asked, frowning at her.

"Line," she replied.

"Oh."

Amanda gave it a few more minutes, then made a show of looking at the clock on her phone.

"I gotta blaze," she said. "My parents will probably be calling looking for me."

She turned to leave, only to bump into Kyle. As she stepped away from him, she could smell a strange kind of odour on him. It wasn't the same as earlier.

Kyle smiled at her, reaching out a hand to steady her. "Where are you going?" he asked, sounding almost friendly toward her. Amanda frowned at him, wondering why the sudden change in mood. He looked almost … happy.

"Her parents might be checking up on her," Lori said.

Kyle rolled his eyes. "Yeah, I hate that. My olds are the same."

Amanda shrugged. "It's their version of tough love," she replied.

Both Kyle and Jake nodded knowingly. Amanda was sure they had not only caught the implication but they'd also been checking up on her.

God, she hoped her cover was good enough. Jim had been dubious when she had told him what she had come up with, but he'd gone along with it anyway.

Amanda Carter had supposedly been kicked out of school for drug possession and sent to rehab before being sent to board with a friend of a friend in the city. The principal at St Anne's had complied with Jim's request for the fake file, although she had been more than a little concerned at what she was undertaking.

Still, if it kept the students from learning her real identity, Amanda decided it was the best option.

Chapter Ten

Jim grumbled as he reached for his phone on the bedside cabinet. It had been vibrating off and on for the last few minutes, letting him know he had a text message.

He yawned and looked blearily at the screen. Thanks to his flatmates' party he hadn't got to bed until nearly three in the morning. According to the clock on his phone, it wasn't even nine yet.

"You'd think she'd know I'm off duty," he grumbled, seeing he had a text from Amanda.

Yo, get ur lazy but out of bed and meet me at Arts Cent. Ten.

"Women!"

Torn between wanting to go back to sleep for another hour or two and wanting to know what her Royal Pain In The Ass wanted. He read the text message again, frowning.

"Arts Cent? What the hell is that?"

He sent a text back, asking her what she was

talking about. The reply came back quickly.

R u an idiot? The arts centre!

There was an art gallery along with some art studios for local artists near the centre of town. The gallery was housed on an estate which had once been a farm that had spread for several thousand acres. The land had been slowly sold off and subdivided as the city had spread further, but the local council had voted to reserve that part of the old estate to provide some culture to the area.

Yawning, Jim threw back the bedcovers and stumbled out to the shower. His flatmates had a huge master bedroom on the second storey of the house so the part he lived in was fairly private. Considering the late hours he usually worked, that was a good thing in his opinion.

Once showered and dressed, he figured he had time for a coffee. The arts centre was about a fifteen-minute drive away.

Just as he'd poured himself a cup of freshly brewed coffee, Craig came down the stairs and stumbled in. His hair was all over the place and his lower jaw was dark with stubble.

"It's way too early for this," he grumbled.

Jim shrugged and poured him a coffee.

"What time did you guys get to bed?"

His flatmate shrugged and tousled his hair, making it stick up even more. He picked up the mug and sipped the black liquid, grimacing.

"Four? Five?" He didn't sound too sure, but then he'd had a lot to drink from what Jim had observed.

"Why're you up so early?"

"Got a meeting," he said. Despite having told his flatmates the basics of what he was doing with Amanda, he didn't want to tell them the meeting was with her.

"Thought you had the weekend off?"

Jim shrugged again. "No such thing when you're a cop."

Craig nodded. "Yeah, I hear that." He frowned. "You're not having breakfast?"

"Got to be at the meeting at ten," he said.

"It's not even nine-thirty!" his flatmate protested.

"I know. I'll grab a protein bar on the way."

"That's no way to eat," his friend protested.

Lesleigh would probably tell him the same thing. He loved his stepmother dearly, but she was something of a worrywart.

He leaned on the counter as he drank his coffee, his senses slowly becoming more alert. Craig finished his own coffee, muttering that he was going back to bed for a bit before stumbling back out to the hallway. Jim heard the stairs creak slightly as his flatmate went to join his partner in the master bedroom.

He glanced at the clock on the microwave. It was nine thirty-five. He put his cup in the sink and went back to his room to grab his keys and phone before leaving the house.

He stopped off at the local dairy and grabbed a protein bar, then continued on to the art centre. There were a few cars parked in the parking area.

More than usual, he thought as he parked his car alongside a Pajero. He wrinkled his nose at the bigger vehicle. His own Corolla sedan wasn't exactly small, but was still dwarfed by the other car. The paint was shiny with that just-out-of-the-showroom look except for the fact that the letters and numbers on the registration plate signified the car was at least four years old.

He huffed in annoyance. It seemed to be the trend in the city that people who were fairly well-off tended to buy off-road vehicles without any intention of actually using them off-road. He'd been to a few accidents where the vehicle had rolled because the driver didn't know how to compensate for the higher centre of gravity. Modern versions were more stable, but Jim was still annoyed by the trend.

He headed into the centre, noticing a sign proclaiming an open day. He'd been wondering why Amanda had chosen such a place to meet and now understood. Given the number of people already here, he realised she couldn't have chosen a better venue. It was public and reasonably crowded so there was less chance of them being recognised.

That was pretty smart thinking on her part, he thought.

Since she hadn't told him specifically where to meet her, he chose the gallery. As luck would have it, she was in the main room, looking at a piece of art that Jim couldn't even begin to interpret. It was a sculpture of some sort, looking a little like some

Maori carvings Jim had seen.

As he began to approach her, he noticed a man checking her out. The man was probably in his late forties, with salt-and-pepper hair and a few creases around his eyes. He was gazing at Amanda with an appreciative look, his mouth upturned in a slight smirk.

The man stepped toward her, his expression showing his intent. Jim got there first, shooting the man a look telling him to back off.

"Hi honey," he said, laying what he hoped looked like a possessive hand on the small of her back.

Amanda turned her head and looked at him, raising an eyebrow. Honey? she mouthed before shifting her gaze to the man who had turned away dejected. She nodded and returned her attention to the sculpture.

He stood with her for a moment, gazing at the sculpture.

"Uh, what is it?"

"Read the card."

He glanced at it. The artist had called it River, but it didn't look like a river to him. It was a stone carving. On top was a spiral of some description and the rest he supposed was meant to represent tributaries. It didn't resemble a river to him. It just looked like random shapes thrown together.

"I don't get it."

"You're not meant to get it," Amanda replied. "It's an abstract."

"A what now?"

She sighed and shook her head. "Heathen." He followed her as she made her way through the gallery. She was clearly interested in the art.

"I suppose you know all about this art stuff," he said.

"I took art history at school. Even thought about studying it at university, but ..." She shrugged. "Can't afford to go and I didn't want to get in debt doing it."

"So ... why here?" he asked.

She rolled her eyes at him. "Duh! Do you really see a bunch of scruffy teenagers coming to look at art?"

"Well, no, but didn't you remind me just the other day that you're still technically a teenager?"

"What does that have to do with anything? So I appreciate art. So what?"

He raised his hands in surrender.

"Okay, you don't have to get on your high horse about it."

"I'm not on my ... whatever! Just keep up and try and look at least a little interested." He nodded and continued to follow her. "By the way," she said quietly. "Thanks. For that guy I mean."

So she had noticed the older guy checking her out and judging from her tone he had either been staring for a while or had been following her.

"He was starting to creep me out," she added.

"Does that happen a lot?" he asked.

She shrugged. "You tell me."

From that he took it to mean it did happen fairly frequently. Amanda was an attractive young woman. It was inevitable that a girl with her looks would attract that kind of attention. At least she was aware of it even if it was unwelcome.

He was surprised that she had even thanked him, given her attitude toward him. Especially after what had happened a few days earlier. Rather than call her on it, he decided to let it go.

She led the way out of the gallery to a caravan where they were selling coffees.

"Want one?" she asked.

"Yeah, thanks," he replied. "Bit of a late night last night."

"Me too," she said. "I didn't get in until two."

"You seem remarkably refreshed for someone who's had about six hours' sleep."

"Actually four," she told him, paying for the coffees and handing him his cup. "I spent a couple of hours working on some notes. For my report," she added.

"Report? Oh, the case." He frowned at her. "Why eight?"

"I went to the gym. Have to keep in shape."

He looked her over with a small smile.

"Well, you're definitely in great shape."

She looked at him over the rim of her coffee cup.

"Are you flirting with me, Mr Andersen?"

"You're kidding, right? I don't flirt."

"You were so flirting."

Okay, maybe I was, he thought, but I'm not about

to admit that. The truth was, when she wasn't acting spoiled, she actually showed glimpses of a girl he wanted to get to know.

"So, what happened last night?" he asked, remembering she had been getting ready to go out when he'd dropped by her place after work.

She told him about going to a local bar that she had overheard the kids talking about. From what he'd seen of the kids' records, only one of them was over eighteen. Which had to mean they'd used fake i.d.s. Sure, that was a crime, but certainly not damning evidence.

"Anyway, I followed these guys and I'm pretty sure they were at least smoking weed. It smelled like it."

"How would you know what weed smells like?" he asked.

"I went to a concert last year and people were smoking it." She screwed up her nose. "Sometimes it smells like burning grass. When I was a kid we had this neighbour who used to put all his grass clippings into an old metal drum and burn it. Of course, then the council found out about it and made him get rid of it. But yeah, it kind of smelled like that. Or like burnt coffee beans. There was something else though. I mean, Kyle, he clearly doesn't like or trust me, but when he came back from outside it was like he was a completely different person."

"In what way?"

"He was friendly. Happy even."

"Well, meth does induce feelings of euphoria. Still, by itself, it's not exactly conclusive. I do think you have good instincts with this guy though."

She raised an eyebrow at him. "Well there's a shocker. You mean I've actually done something right for a change?"

"Don't knock it Princess. Trust me, compliments will be few and far between until you can prove to me you're actually capable of doing the job you were sent to do."

She huffed. "Oh come on, it's not like I can actually go walking up to Kyle and ask him: 'are you dealing drugs?' I mean, geez, that kind of thing happens in the movies, not in real life."

"I know what it's like," he responded. "Trust me, you get some guys who go to police college and think it's like it is on a tv cop show. You find the evidence just like that," he added, snapping his fingers, "and you get the bad guys all within an hour of prime time." He rolled his eyes.

Amanda grinned. "My dad hates those shows. When I was a kid he was always complaining about how unrealistic they are and I keep telling him that the reality just doesn't make for good drama on tv."

Jim laughed. "Oh yeah. I think if there was ever a show that did nothing but follow a cop all day, people would turn off in droves."

Amanda nodded her agreement. They both looked at each other for a long moment. Jim smiled at her. For a moment it seemed as if they had found some common ground.

"Um, anyway, I saved the notes on a flash drive." She took the small drive from her purse and handed it to him. "Just some of my observations and stuff."

"I'm sure it's fine."

"Uh, there's something else you should know. One of the kids saw me with you. If they figure out you're a cop, they might just think I'm a narc."

"And blow your cover?" He nodded. That could certainly be complicated. Of course, the main problem was there really wasn't enough evidence for them to arrest anyone or bring one of the kids in for questioning.

He thought about what she had said on the way home and realised she had been meaning the night in the café. That explained her behaviour that night, he thought, recalling the families dining. Maybe one of them had included the kid she'd told him about.

While he felt she could have handled it another way, she was right to be concerned. If one of the kids were to figure it out, it could put her in a very bad situation.

He would figure out a way to get around the problem. Somehow.

Chapter Eleven

The rest of the weekend was thankfully uneventful. Amanda had spent some of her time catching up on the latest gossip with her friend Kerry, who kept asking questions about her and Jim. She assured her friend there was really nothing to tell, not that Kerry actually believed her. According to her friend, half the sworn staff at the station thought there was something other than business going on between her and the detective.

Amanda snorted to herself. For cops, they seemed to thrive on the latest gossip.

The remainder of the weekend she spent trying to come up with a way to solve the case without getting caught. She wished there was a way for her to listen in on conversations without actually having to be present. There was something about Kyle and his friends that she didn't like, although Lori seemed nice. If circumstances had been different, Amanda thought she could have actually been friends with the girl.

As she'd complained to Jim it wasn't like in the movies where the investigator had access to the latest in modern technology. Her bosses weren't exactly raking in the money, relying on good old-fashioned legwork to get the job done. Listening devices were great, but not everyone had access to such things, she thought.

She went in to work for a couple of hours on Sunday, figuring she could use the peace and quiet of the office instead of having to put up with her flatmate's bad taste in music. Amanda didn't mind some rap and hip-hop, but since most of the stuff her flatmate listened to tended to be heavily laced with profanity or the so-called artist screaming the lyrics, she would rather not be around it.

She snorted at the thought of what Jim would say to that. At least she had taste, she reminded herself.

"Amanda? What are you doing here?"

She looked up from the laptop and frowned at her silver-haired boss. Jerry Knight wasn't as fit as his business partner. He had a stocky build with what most described as a beer belly.

"Mr Knight?"

"Shouldn't you be out enjoying the sun?" he asked.

It was a sunny day outside, but winter was coming and the warm days would become a rarity for the next few months.

"Oh, I just wanted to do a couple of hours' work while I had the chance. My flatmate can be kind of, um, loud." She explained about the rap music.

He laughed softly. "Ah yes, I remember those days. Hindsight does allow for some selectiveness and we do tend to be kinder in our memory than what we actually experienced."

He came in and sat down in the chair opposite her desk.

"When I first came to live here after completing my training, I shared a house with another constable and two of his friends. This was back in the days when music was actually music, not like it is today." He winked at her. "I suppose I sound like an old fuddy duddy."

She shook her head. "Not in the slightest. My dad loves music from the sixties and seventies and I guess he passed it down to me."

"There were times when I was desperate for my own space. Four people living in a small house tended to live in each other's pockets, so to speak. I don't know how people do it these days," he added with a sigh. "But then I suppose they do it out of necessity." He started to get up. "I'm interrupting your work."

"You don't have to go," she told him, enjoying the opportunity to get to know her boss a little.

In the six months she had worked at the small agency, this was the first time the former police detective had actually sat down and shared anything of his life with her. She had thought him aloof and rather distant, but now she sensed that he was kind of reserved. He at least seemed kind, which was something of a change compared to Bob Moody.

"How is your investigation going?" he asked.

"Not well," she said. "I get the impression Mr Donaldson expected the case would be over already."

Her boss shook his head.

"Sadly, our clients do tend to have fairly high expectations, but they also need to realise that such things can take time. For instance, I've been working on a potential adultery case. I've been following this man around for two weeks and have yet to catch him doing anything untoward. That isn't to say that he isn't cheating, just that he seems to be able to avoid getting caught."

"I guess cases like that are pretty much the norm for a p.i.," she said.

"Oh trust me, it isn't like you see on television. I certainly don't have it as easy as Thomas Magnum, although sometimes I think I'd probably get the adventure and the girls if I looked like him," looking down at himself and laughing ruefully.

Amanda laughed with him, reminded of the same conversation she had had with Jim the day before. It had been nice to actually share a laugh with him. When he wasn't being condescending, he seemed like a fairly nice guy.

"I've actually been sitting here wondering what I'm supposed to do next."

"Amanda, your job is to observe, take notes and see where they lead. I happen to think you're a very capable young woman. I'm certain you will figure it out."

She smiled at her boss as he got up from the chair.

"Thank you," she said.

He smiled back. "You're welcome."

When she returned to the school the next day, she was determined not to miss a thing. She spent less time pretending to pay attention to the teachers and more time observing her fellow students.

Kyle and Jake appeared to notice her behaviour. Every time they caught her watching them she affected a bored expression and slouched in her chair. The youths smirked at her and turned back to whatever they had been doing.

As the days passed and her notebook filled with her observations, Amanda began to see that Donaldson had been right about one thing. There was something brewing in the school, but drugs were only the tip of the iceberg.

What she had noted was an undercurrent around the school. She wouldn't go so far as to call it fear, but it was clear that a certain group of students seemed to think they held dominion over the rest of the student body. Kyle and Jake were part of that group.

She would be sitting watching them at certain times when another student would approach, only to give them a wide berth, shooting them an uneasy look.

Like every school, Fraley had its divisive cliques,

from the ones called nerds or geeks to the school athletes. Yet even those who were considered to be potential sports stars avoided Kyle's group like the plague.

Lori seemed to be the only aberration. While she appeared to dislike Kyle, she still hung out with him. It was something Amanda couldn't understand.

She was leaving the grounds one afternoon and headed toward the back gate when Lori grabbed her arm.

"Don't go that way," she said.

Amanda looked at her. "What? Why? What's going on?"

"Nothing. Just don't go that way. Come on."

Amanda glanced uneasily toward the gate where she could see some of the students gathering. Something was definitely going on. As much as she wanted to know what it was, she had to let Lori lead her away or else arouse the girl's suspicions.

Determined to find out exactly what was happening and why, she left a message for Jim to contact her. She hung out with Lori for a while until she could make an excuse and get away. She got back to the office to find a message to call her father.

"Dad?"

"Hi honey. Jim got your message but he's a little preoccupied right now."

"Why? What's going on?" she asked, remembering she'd asked Lori that same question.

"There was some kind of altercation at the school.

Our uniformed guys are still trying to talk to witnesses. I'm afraid Jim's going to be tied up with this all night."

"That was kind of what I wanted to talk to him about. This happened in McCallister Street, didn't it? It's where the back gate leads."

"Yeah, it did honey. Why? You know something?"

"Not really. I was headed that way but Lori pulled me away. She wouldn't tell me what was going on, but I'm sure Kyle and Jake were involved." She had told her father what she had observed so far.

"Do you think she knew what they had planned?"

"I don't know, Dad. She knew something, that's for sure."

The incident was all over school the next day. It was like Chinese Whispers, Amanda thought. Everyone seemed to think they knew something but they all had different versions of what went down. What Amanda did manage to put together from the various accounts was that one of the school's star athletes had confronted one of the kids in Kyle's group, accusing him of sleeping with his girlfriend. A fight had ensued and the athlete was now in the hospital, fighting for his life.

Amanda was forced to pretend she didn't care about the fight. She wanted to know more, but she also needed to keep an eye on Kyle. He was trying to hide it, but he was hurt. She could see him wincing every time he sat down, a clear indication that he had bruised ribs at least. Even if Kyle hadn't instigated the fight, he had definitely participated.

"Amanda, report to the principal's office."

Frowning, Amanda stared at the visitor to the classroom. Once a week, a Year Nine student was chosen at random to be a runner for the school office. She barely remembered being thirteen herself but she didn't remember looking so small and frightened of her own shadow as the thirteen-year-old standing beside the teacher did.

She glanced at Kyle and rolled her eyes, sighing as if the call to the office was a major inconvenience. She huffed and grabbed her things, following the young boy out of the classroom and down the corridor to the school's administration building.

The principal's assistant waved her in, telling the boy, Josh, to go back to his seat and his book. Amanda ignored the woman and entered the office, surprised to see Jim there, along with a uniformed constable. Donaldson was sitting at his desk, his face white.

"What is it?" she asked.

"Mitchell Cole just died," the principal replied.

Chapter Twelve

Jim bit his lip as Amanda's face turned white in shock. She appeared to take a long, deep breath, letting it out slowly.

"What ..." Her voice sounded hoarse. She coughed. "What happened?"

"That's what we were hoping you could tell us," the uniformed officer replied. "Detective Andersen told me what you were doing here."

Jim glanced at the constable.

"Oh, Stu Dawson, Amanda Steele. She's using the last name Carter here."

"We've met, sort of," Amanda told him, glancing at the senior constable with an unreadable expression. Given the man's reputation around the station, Jim wasn't surprised she knew of him at least.

Amanda shook her head. "I don't know much. All I've been able to glean so far is that Cole accused one of Kyle's friends of sleeping with his girlfriend."

Jim nodded. That was as much as he'd been able to get from the single witness who had come forward. The young man had been scared, almost too intimidated to say anything, but Mitchell had been his friend. That alone had been sufficient to make him come forward.

"You sure there isn't anything else?" Dawson asked.

"Well, I do know one of the guys appears to be hurt. Probably bruised ribs."

"Who?" Jim asked.

"Kyle," she said, looking at the principal.

Donaldson nodded. "I can pull up his student record."

Jim shook his head. "Not necessary. I know who she's talking about and I have a fairly thick file on him already."

The principal looked at him with surprise in his expression. "Oh, you do?"

"I've been keeping up with this since Amanda's father asked me to keep an eye on things." He raised his hand as the man looked as if he was about to object. "We're not here to interfere with Amanda's investigation, just back her up if things get dodgy. That's all."

Donaldson still looked dubious. Jim glanced at Amanda as she spoke up.

"Mr Donaldson … Matt … I know you didn't really want the police involved but at this point, I think they have to be." She paused. "You were right when you said there was something very wrong at this school and I don't think we've even scratched the surface. I mean, never mind the kids. The parents and the school board are just turning a blind eye and it makes me wonder if some of them are just as involved."

"That's a rather bold accusation," Dawson told her. For once he wasn't behaving like the complete narcissist he was and actually seemed to be taking her seriously.

Jim had to agree with Amanda when he thought about the situation a little later. There were some parents who had powerful connections, despite the fact they lived in a poor area. He knew of at least two families who were affiliated with the local gangs. Another, he was fairly sure had connections in Wellington.

Those connections weren't going to keep the truth from coming out, he thought. There was definitely something brewing at the school. Amanda had likened it to a charged atmosphere right before a bad storm, but it was more than that. Jim was sure it was all about to blow up in their faces.

In the meantime, he had a boy's death to investigate. So far, it all looked like an accident, but he wasn't so sure. Only the coroner's report would give him more conclusive results.

He decided to call the boy's girlfriend and get her in for an interview. The girl, also a student at Fraley High, came in looking tearful. She was a pretty girl of barely sixteen with long red hair down to her waist.

Her hand shook as she pushed a lock of hair away from her face.

"Sit down, Miss ..."

"Emma," she said quietly. Her voice sounded hoarse. Jim noticed her eyes were puffy and her face was pale.

"Emma, tell me about Mitchell. Were you close?"

She nodded. "We've known each other since we were ten. Knew each other," she added, looking stricken.

"Mitchell accused another boy of sleeping with you. Is that true?"

She looked up at him, her blue eyes wide.

"Uh ... s-sorry. I don't know what you ..."

"Did you sleep with this other boy?"

"I - I didn't ..." she said. Her expression changed. Jim was given the impression she was afraid of something. "I mean, yes, I ..."

A single tear slipped down her cheek. Jim grabbed a box of tissues and handed it to her, watching silently as she began to cry before pulling out a handful of tissues and blowing her nose. He waited for her to gain some control.

"Emma, you're not in trouble here. We just want to know what really happened between your boyfriend and this other boy."

"I don't know what happened," she said. "Mitch told me to stay away. He said he was going to teach the guy a lesson."

That pretty much tallied with what the dead youth's friend had told him, Jim thought. Mitchell Cole had started the fight but he clearly hadn't counted on there being more than one opponent. That had led to the boy's death.

He tried to get more out of the girl, but she would break down every few minutes and it became almost pointless trying to get anything coherent from her. Jim let her go, but not before making sure she would be available again if he needed to ask more questions.

As he was working on his notes from the aborted interview, his boss stopped by his desk.

"How's it going?" Pete asked.

"Honestly? It's not. I could barely get any sense out of the girl. There was something though. I just can't quite put my finger on what exactly."

"Maybe I can help," the sergeant suggested.

"I don't know." Jim sighed. "Okay, well, I asked the girl if she had slept with this other guy. I thought for a moment she was going to deny it, but ... I don't know. She seemed afraid for some reason."

Pete frowned. "Hmm, that does sound a bit off. What's Amanda's take on all this?"

"I think she feels the same way I do. There is something not right at that school. Something ... I don't know ... I don't want to sound like a walking cliché, but something evil. God, I can't believe I said that," he moaned, rubbing a hand over his eyes.

"In your opinion, is Amanda safe, or should we pull her out of there?"

He looked at his boss. "Uh, isn't that more your concern than mine? You're her father."

"That's the problem. I don't want to think I'm over-reacting."

Jim considered this. Had their positions been reversed, he probably would feel the same way. Still, in spite of her immaturity, Amanda was the only one who could know for sure whether she was in any danger or not. He didn't want to think about how she would take it if he did make her pull out.

"Right now, there isn't enough evidence to decide. I think she's okay, for now, but yeah, if things get worse, I think we should seriously consider it."

He decided to keep looking further into the parents, thinking there had to be some connection somewhere. He read the report from Dawson, who had been talking to another witness, but there was nothing conclusive there.

It all smacked of some sort of cover-up. Donaldson was doing his best, but it felt as if someone else was trying to make it go away.

He called Amanda but she wasn't picking up her cell phone. He tried the main phone at her flat but her flatmate picked up.

"Hello?"

"Is Amanda there?"

"No. Who's this?"

"A ... friend."

"What sort of friend?" the girl asked in a tone that sounded suspiciously like a purr.

"A none of your business sort of friend," he replied, not liking the other girl's manner. Her tone immediately changed direction.

"Geez, no need to get snarky," she replied, sounding annoyed. "Amanda's at work."

"Well, when do you expect her back?"

"I dunno." The young woman sounded put out. "I'm not her keeper am I?"

There was the sound of a door closing and the flatmate called out.

"Oh hey, there's some jerk on the phone asking for you."

Jim waited a few seconds as there were slightly muffled voices, then he heard the static as the handset was exchanged.

"Hi Jim."

"How'd you know it was me?" he asked.

"I'm psychic?" she replied, snickering. "Duh, we have caller i.d." He let that one slide.

"We need to talk about today."

She was quiet for a moment. When she spoke again, her tone was cool, but not unfriendly. "Yeah, I guess we do. Okay, how long will it take you to drive here?"

"Twenty minutes, give or take."

"You eaten?"

"Not yet," he replied.

"Well, I was going to grab some Chinese for dinner. It's takeaways night."

"You know that's really …" He was going to say 'bad for you' but he wasn't in the mood to argue with her. It seemed she read his mind anyway.

"This place I go to, they don't use MSG. Their meals are actually a lot healthier than some places. And they make a really mean sweet-and-sour pork."

"Okay. How about you call in the order and I'll pick it up on my way. Where is this place?"

"It's on the corner of Kentigern Street and Adams Place. You can't miss it. I'll see you shortly."

Chapter Thirteen

Amanda made sure the flat was at least reasonably tidy. Her flatmate Penny was a bit of a slob and hated cleaning up after herself.

Penny had gone to her room after Amanda had taken the call. She came out while putting her hair up in a messy bun. She frowned, watching as Amanda picked up some of the rubbish Penny had left on the coffee table.

"What are you doing?"

"What does it look like I'm doing?" she retorted. "Cleaning up your mess! Honestly, I don't know how you managed to get to twenty-four and still be such a slob."

Penny shrugged. "So? Who is this guy anyway?"

"None of your business," Amanda returned.

"Yeah, that's what he said. So?"

Amanda sighed. "He works with my father and he's helping me with something to do with work."

"Oh." Penny shrugged as she opened the front door and lit a cigarette. Amanda scrunched up her nose in disgust.

"Why do you always have to do that?"

"Well, where else am I gonna do it?" her flatmate replied. "You won't let me smoke inside!"

"It's on the tenancy," Amanda replied, sighing. "You knew that when you signed up for this place."

"I hate that," Penny grumbled. "It's like they're trying to force smokers to quit or something."

"Or something," Amanda told her. Her friend sighed heavily. "Oh, come on. It's not like you didn't know that was exactly what the government was trying to achieve when they introduced the smoking ban."

Penny stared at her for a moment, taking a puff of her cigarette before removing the butt from her mouth and pointing it at her, wisps of smoke rising from the tip.

"You know, sometimes you sound like a teenager and sometimes you sound older than I am."

"Whatever," Amanda muttered.

She knew there were times when she could sound hopelessly immature, but Penny wasn't wrong. Amanda had long since recognised that she tended to act older than most people her age because she had been practically independent from the night her mother had left. Her father had tried to let her be a kid as long as possible, but she had always known his job was just as important, if not more so than her. Which meant she only had herself to rely on.

That wasn't to say she didn't do dumb things

from time to time. She was only nineteen. By some standards she was still considered too young for various things, like signing up for study at university or the local technical institute. That still required her father's signature on the paperwork. Yet it was ironic that from the age of eighteen she could vote and buy alcohol for herself.

She heard a car pull up in the driveway and glanced through the window, spotting Jim's Corolla. Penny seemed to perk up when she saw him getting out of the car.

"You didn't say it was him."

Amanda frowned at her flatmate. She'd forgotten that Penny had met the detective nearly a week earlier.

"Like I said, none of your business," she told her.

"How old is he, anyway? He's kinda hot."

"Is he?" she asked. "I didn't notice," she lied.

Penny greeted Jim with a smile.

"Hi," she said, sticking her hand out. "I don't believe we were properly introduced last week.

Amanda rolled her eyes. When Penny was trying to show-off, she really went all out. "Jim Andersen, Penny Cameron."

"Ooh, food," Penny replied. The brunette's eyes lit up as she saw the bags of Chinese.

"I only ordered enough for me and Jim. You said you were going out tonight."

Brown eyes gazed at her before turning back to practically devour Jim. Okay so the guy was good-looking, Amanda thought. Her flatmate didn't have to act like a she-wolf in heat for crying out loud!

"Did I? When did I say that?"

"This morning. As I was leaving for work."

"Oh. Yeah, I guess I did say that." She shrugged. "It was just a date with a guy I was set up with. He'll probably chicken out."

Amanda shot a desperate look at Jim. It wasn't that she didn't trust her flatmate but the last thing she wanted to do was try to talk to Jim about the case with her butting in trying to flirt with him. As much as she liked her friend, Penny was one of those young women who seemed to think the world revolved around her.

A few months earlier Amanda had let her friend drag her to a local nightclub; not that it had really been that hard. Amanda could be old-fashioned on some things but she still liked to party. Once at the club, Penny had begun flirting with a group of guys. As soon as it became clear one of them had only been interested in Amanda, Penny had dragged her away. It had been completely irrelevant that Amanda hadn't been as interested in the guy as he had been in her. Penny had been livid.

Jim smiled at Penny, which the woman took to be encouragement to continue sidling up to him, smiling flirtatiously.

"Actually, Amanda and I have some business things to discuss."

Penny pouted. Amanda rolled her eyes. Really? she thought. Did the woman really think that would work?

On second thought, she could see Jim practically drooling. So her flatmate was model-gorgeous. Did he really have to make those eyes at her?

"What kind of business?" Penny asked, sounding put out. "I'm 2-i-c at my office. I could …"

"Police business," Jim told her. "Besides, I'd hate to be that guy you were supposed to meet tonight. I'd certainly hate to miss out on a date with such a gorgeous woman."

Penny appeared to re-think her strategy. Of course she was flattered by the compliment, but still torn between staying and flirting some more with Jim or going out.

"All right," she said. She turned and wrapped an arm around Amanda's shoulders, squeezing hard enough to break the bones of a less solid woman. "Play nice now. Don't do anything I wouldn't do."

Amanda nodded, knowing the squeeze, meant to look friendly in front of Jim, was really a hands-off warning from her flatmate.

Penny went back to her room to change, giving Jim a wink and deliberately brushing her hand over the fabric of his jacket. Amanda waited until the woman had left the room before grabbing Jim's arm.

"Seriously? Close your mouth. You're drooling!"

She grabbed the bag of food from him and took it into the kitchen, leaving him to make himself at home.

"Nice place," he called out as she pulled the container out of the paper bag and began dishing out the food on plates.

"It's all right," she replied.

The flat wasn't all that bad, although it tended to be freezing in winter. The landlord was reluctant to install insulation, despite the government's measures to help tenants by forcing owners to do so. He'd also never bothered to install any kind of heating and the electric appliances they did use didn't help.

Penny had found the house through a real estate website and had signed up to rent the place without considering Amanda's views on the subject. Amanda didn't like to complain, but her flatmate could be a little self-centred at times.

She did have her moments however. When Penny wasn't being selfish, she was actually a good friend and a good listener. Amanda had met her through Penny's brother, Lucas, who she'd gone to school with. Lucas had shared a place with his sister until he'd decided to enrol at Canterbury University and had suggested Amanda take over his room when she'd decided to move out of home.

When Penny had been promoted and given a raise, she had decided to find a better place out of the inner city. The place was only marginally better than the apartment they'd shared in the CBD.

The house was small with only two bedrooms, the larger being Penny's of course. She had a sliding door out to the deck and a double wardrobe, while Amanda was stuck with a single wardrobe and a room that she did not consider to be large enough to fit a double bed and her small amount of bedroom furniture.

The one advantage to the place was that it was reasonably cheap in rent, compared to a lot of other places nearby. The owner had bought the old villa and renovated it with the intention of living in it himself, but a job offer in another part of the country had meant he never actually did get to live there.

Jim came into the kitchen.

"You don't like the place?"

Amanda shrugged. "It's okay. It's got its good points and bad points."

"What good points?"

"It's cheap," she said.

"And bad points?"

"Well, the money I save on rent, I spend on commuting and parking. I mean, it's so far out it takes me an hour to get to work. At least an hour and a half if I take the train."

He nodded. "Yeah, I can see how that would be a disadvantage."

Amanda finished dishing out the food and placed the container in the sink.

"Don't you just throw those out?" Jim asked.

She shrugged. "They're good for food storage," she said.

"Oh. So, drinks?"

"There's some Sprite in the fridge. No booze, sorry."

"That's okay. I don't like to drink when I'm

driving," he said, grabbing a couple of glasses from the shelf and the bottle from the fridge. "Better safe than sorry."

She glanced at him, nodding. "I guess being a cop you've seen it all anyway."

"Well, you'd know, I guess. With your dad."

They walked back out to the living room. Jim sat on the couch while Amanda sat on the loveseat. They'd barely begun digging into their meals when Penny came out, dressed in a short skirt that showed off her long, slim legs. Her blouse was sleeveless and seemed to shimmer in the light. She'd made up her face, using bold lines and shadows to emphasise her eyes and thick mascara. She was forever telling Amanda to wear more make-up but Amanda had always preferred a more natural look.

"Don't wait up," she told Amanda before rushing out the door.

Chapter Fourteen

Jim snorted to himself. The two girls couldn't have been more disparate if they tried. Amanda, while fairly self-confident, didn't flaunt her attractiveness. Penny was pretty, he would give her that, but he had never been the type of man to go for such shallowness. It was also fairly clear that Penny thought all men should flock to her and ignore her flatmate.

Amanda probably didn't think he saw, but he could tell she wasn't happy at the other girl's attitude. They might not be friends, but he liked her enough to refuse to dis her by flirting with her flatmate. He'd only said what he had to get rid of the woman.

Amanda might pretend she didn't care, but he knew only too well how it felt to have someone he thought was a friend show such disrespect. It had happened to him a few times.

"So, what did you want to talk about?" Amanda asked.

"We didn't get much chance to discuss things in Donaldson's office. Have you seen or heard anything that might cause you to suspect there's more to this kid's death than a fight?"

She shook her head. "Everyone was talking about it at the school, but I don't think they really know what's happening. Those who do aren't talking at all."

"What about you? What's your feeling on this?"

She took a forkful of the food and chewed thoughtfully before replying.

"There's something that isn't being said. Maybe I'm imagining it ..."

"But you don't think so?" he prompted.

"You know that feeling you get when the hairs on the back of your neck stand up? That's kind of the way I'm feeling around these kids. Especially Kyle. I really don't like the guy but I couldn't say why I don't like him. It could just be that he's a jerk ..."

"He's had a few run-ins, but mostly over drug possession and D.U.I.s," Jim told her. "No violence offences. According to his father, he's supposed to have cleaned up his act."

"Not from what I saw the other night."

Kyle's father was either lying or completely ignorant about his son's activities. The parents were divorced and the father had custody. Jim had learnt the man worked as a solicitor, defending mostly petty crime cases. While he claimed he made a fairly decent income, they lived in a small house that had once been a government rental property - one of those that had been part of a few sold off some years earlier.

Of course it could be possible that the man had to pay spousal support to his ex-wife. She was not exactly a pleasant woman to deal with either, Jim thought, recalling a report from an interview with the mother when Kyle had first begun getting into trouble. The mother had been belligerent, suggesting that the police had falsified evidence to accuse her son. She clearly had no respect for police.

Kyle was no doubt smart enough to know right from wrong. He was arrogant and clearly needed some decent discipline, but his parents were either too reluctant or too scared to do so. He had been sent to juvenile detention at fourteen for mouthing off to the judge after being caught smoking marijuana at school. He was a kid who was headed for a life in and out of prison unless he cleaned up his act.

"Don't worry," he said. "I get it. There is something really wrong at that school. I think Donaldson may be in over his head. Now my question to you is, are you in over your head?"

She pushed her plate away, clearly considering it.

"It's a fair question," she said. "I mean, I could take it the wrong way and think you're just saying that because you don't think I can do the job, but I think you're really worried about this. Do I think there's a danger there? Yes. Should I pull out? Part of me thinks that would be the smartest decision, but I'm my father's daughter. I'm stubborn enough to feel that to do so would be to let them win. Donaldson needs help, Jim, and maybe I'm the only one to do it."

"Even if we're now fully involved?"

She looked at him, her expression thoughtful.

"Jim, that school is going to close unless Donaldson manages to turn it around enough to satisfy the Ministry. From what I can see, most of those kids are innocent. There's just a certain element that thinks they can control everything, from the kids to the teachers. If we, I mean, I can get enough evidence to put these kids away, Donaldson might just have a chance to save the school."

"You really believe in this, don't you?" he asked.

She sighed. "I have to admit, even I had my doubts going into this. I wondered if there was anything left to save, but now ... Donaldson's right. If he's not willing to stand up and say 'enough' who will? And it's my job to make sure that happens."

He had to admire her tenacity. He might have considered it arrogance, or over-confidence, but he now understood that Amanda was just trying to do the right thing, no matter how potentially dangerous it was.

He just hoped it didn't turn to custard. Something told him the worst was yet to come.

At the station the next day, his boss asked him for an update. Jim sat in the sergeant's office, reluctant to even mention the discussion with Amanda.

Pete looked him over, his gaze assessing.

"Amanda called me last night after you left her place. She told me what you'd discussed. Thank you, by the way, for respecting my daughter enough to not insist that she drop this."

"Well, sir, as concerned as I am given the events of the last few days, I think Amanda has the right to decide whether she wants to continue this. I mean, so far, all we have is that this was an accidental death. Despite my instincts telling me there is more to this. I do think Amanda might be in the best position to talk to the kids, maybe get to the bottom of things."

His boss smiled. "That's what I like about you Jim. I know you and Amanda have had a few personality clashes, but you two work well together."

"Your daughter's pretty smart, boss. And I'm not just saying that because she's your daughter."

He understood now why Amanda wanted so badly to join the police. She wasn't looking to follow in her father's footsteps. She genuinely cared about doing the right thing, no matter the cost.

That didn't change his feelings, however. Ever since the boy had died in the hospital, Jim had a huge knot in his stomach. He couldn't help worrying about the girl and what she was letting herself in for.

His worry increased tenfold two days later when he was given the news that another student had died. This time it was far too close for comfort. The dead student had been one of the group Amanda had been trying to get close to.

Chapter Fifteen

Amanda decided to check out the bar again the next night, wondering if Kyle and the others would show up. She didn't see any reason why they wouldn't. As far as Mitchell Cole was concerned, his death was an accident. The police were still investigating of course, but so far all the evidence pointed to his death being the result of a fall.

Lori turned up shortly after eleven. Judging from her expression, she was not happy to see Amanda there.

"What are you doing here?" she asked.

"Needed to get out of the house," Amanda replied with a shrug. "It's kind of suffocating."

Lori looked uneasy, fidgeting as if she needed to go to the bathroom. She was clearly anxious about something.

"Kyle and Jake are gonna be here soon. You shouldn't ..."

"Shouldn't what?" Amanda asked, peering interestedly at her. "Shouldn't be here? Why not?

What's going on Lori?"

"You should stay away from them. Kyle especially."

"Why?" She stared at the girl refusing to budge despite the girl's efforts to push her toward the exit.

"Look, Amanda, I like you, which is why this is the last place you should be. You don't want to get in trouble, especially now. I mean, your parents wouldn't like you hanging around guys like Kyle. He's ... he's bad news and, you know, with your, um, with what happened at your last school ..."

Amanda stared at her, trying to affect an expression of incredulity.

"What about what happened at my last school?" she asked.

"You know," Lori said. She lowered her voice to a loud whisper, leaning close to Amanda. "The school kicked you out because of the drugs."

"How did you know about that?" she asked, widening her eyes, hoping the girl would buy the act.

"Um, somebody told me," Lori muttered.

"Hey girls. What's new?"

Amanda looked at Kyle. He already had a glass in his hand with what looked like beer. The glass was half-full, which meant he'd been in the bar a while. He smiled at her.

"Hey cutie!" he said, leaning in close to her.

She suppressed the urge to gag at the smell of stale cigarette smoke and what she assumed was marijuana coming off him in waves.

Lori's cousin had pulled her aside and was whispering something in her ear. Whatever it was, the brunette did not look happy.

"No!" she said, waving her arm as if to pull away from the youth.

"So Mandy, wanna get a drink?" Kyle pulled out a small scrunched-up wad of notes. Amanda could see the green of the twenty-dollar note as well as the blue of the ten dollar. "My shout," the youth added.

She wanted to refuse but decided to let this play out, asking for a beer. Lori stared at her, shaking her head slightly. Amanda frowned, trying to interpret the girl's mute message, but before she could ask her what was up, her cousin dragged her away.

The bar became even noisier as the music was turned up. Amanda pretended to be interested in watching the dancers on the floor while continuing to watch Lori and Jake. They appeared to be arguing about something as both became progressively more agitated.

A beer was placed in front of her. "There you go," Kyle told her with a smile.

There was that feeling again, Amanda thought. Her gut instinct told her Kyle was planning something. He was acting way too friendly.

Lori shook off her cousin and returned to the table. Amanda wasn't sure how it happened but Lori's arm hit the glass of beer and knocked it over. Beer spilled everywhere, soaking Amanda's shirt. The glass fell on the wooden floor and smashed. People sitting at other tables turned to stare in their direction.

"Oh my god!" Lori squealed. "I'm so sorry!"

Amanda pulled at her soaked shirt. It wasn't that she really wanted the drink but at the same time she didn't want it to get spilled either. Especially with the amount of attention they'd attracted. One of the girls who worked in the bar came over with a cloth and began mopping up the beer from the table, while the young bartender Amanda had spotted with Kyle and Jake the week before also hurried over. He looked at Kyle with an odd expression before bending to pick up the broken glass.

Despite how uncomfortable she was, Amanda couldn't help noticing both Jake and Kyle looked extremely annoyed. Jake once again pulled his cousin away, dragging her through the crowd.

"Let me get you another drink," Kyle said, his hand on her arm as if pulling her out of the way of the staff.

She shook her head. The wet shirt felt more than a little uncomfortable and she smelled like a brewery. She'd also managed to get some of the beer on the front of her pants which was going to be embarrassing.

"No, thanks. I'm just gonna go home."

"I can drive you," he offered.

She again had that feeling that something was off in the way he was behaving. It wasn't like him to be so solicitous. She bit her lip, her every instinct telling her not to trust him.

Fortunately, the clean-up provided a distraction

of sorts and Amanda took advantage of it to slip away from Kyle and out the main door. A taxi driver saw her and pulled up outside.

"Have a little accident?" the man asked kindly in what sounded to her like an Indian accent. He was bearded and covered his hair with a turban.

"Uh, yeah. Can you drive me home please?"

She gave him the address and opted to sit in the back instead of the front, apologising for the state she was in.

"Don't worry about it, miss," he said. "I have had much worse."

As he pulled away from the kerb, Amanda saw Kyle run out of the bar. She sank down in the backseat, hoping he hadn't seen her. The last thing she wanted was for him to follow her home.

The driver chattered to her on the way home. She learnt he had only been in the country a couple of years and was a qualified chef. He was moonlighting as a taxi driver so he could save money to open his own restaurant. He was nice, clearly thinking she was feeling a little distressed by the 'accident' and not expecting too much from her in the way of conversation.

Amanda spent most of the drive going over what had happened. First there was Lori's concern that she 'not be there'. Second, there was Kyle's odd behaviour toward her and his offer to buy her a drink. Third, there was the spilling of the drink. Something nagged at the back of her mind, but she couldn't quite get a handle on what it was.

"I'm really sorry about the shirt," she told the driver as he paused in his chatter.

He smiled and waved his hand. "It's nothing. I have had ladies as young as yourself throw up in the taxi, so this is really not all bad."

She smiled back at him. "Well, thank you for being so understanding. I guess that happens a lot."

He nodded. "There was a young girl not too long ago. I picked her up from the park. She did not look well."

He explained he had picked her up around four in the morning. She had seemed disoriented and more than a little frightened. She'd thrown up in the back of the taxi. While that hadn't been unusual in itself he told her, what was were the contents of what she had thrown up. The man observed that he had never seen pink vomit before.

"Pink?" Amanda asked, frowning.

He nodded. "It was very strange. Perhaps you know of this girl. She was about your age, or younger. Maybe sixteen." He sighed and shook his head. "A girl so young should have more respect for herself."

Amanda nodded distractedly. The driver continued chattering, remarking on the cultural differences and how girls in his culture would never do such things.

He was telling her about having found a cell phone in the taxi while he was cleaning it after the incident when he stopped in her driveway.

Amanda saw the lights weren't on which meant Penny hadn't come home. She had probably gone out partying after work, Amanda thought.

She handed the driver enough to pay for the fare and another twenty dollars to pay toward the cleaning bill. She had no doubt the back seat now smelled just as bad as she did.

"Thank you miss," he said, palming the money. "I hope your night gets better."

"Yours too," she replied.

Once in the house, she stripped off and turned on the shower, rinsing off the beer, which had started to dry and stick to her skin. It was a relief to get rid of the smell which had been making her feel a little nauseated.

Amanda got out of the shower and patted herself dry, going to her bedroom to change into a nightshirt before returning to the bathroom to gather her clothes. Her top was sticky and badly stained from the beer. Amanda sighed and grabbed a plastic bag, intending to toss it in with the rubbish and put the bag in the bin beside the vanity unit.

She went to bed and read for a while, but the incident kept playing over and over in her head. She just couldn't shake the feeling that something bad was about to go down.

She was up late the next day, having spent several hours tossing and turning. She went for a run, hoping that would help clear her mind and ease the tension she was feeling. By the time she returned to the house she was a little less stressed, although she still had no answers as to what had happened.

She was surprised to find her father in the house. A coffee mug sat on the table in front of him. Penny was curled up on the couch watching television.

"Daddy?"

He stood up from the couch and looked at her sombrely. Penny glared at her.

"Next time, take your cell phone," she grumbled before turning back to the television.

Amanda ignored her, approaching her father.

"Dad? What's wrong? You don't normally come here unless ..."

He glanced at her flatmate, then stood up. He took her hand, gently pulling her outside and closing the door.

"Honey, there's no easy way to say this. There was a girl found by the river early this morning. She's been identified as a student at Fraley High."

Amanda frowned at him. Another death? She listened as he explained that a man jogging along the river had found the body of the girl and immediately called police.

"What are you not telling me?" she asked.

He sighed softly. "Honey, I've read your reports. The girl's name is Lori Mattison."

She stared at him, suddenly feeling sick. "What?"

Chapter Sixteen

Jim knelt down on the grass beside the river, trying to get a different perspective of the scene. There was still police tape held in place by pegs surrounding the area where the girl's body had been found five hours earlier. Forensics had already been all over the crime scene and taken away as much evidence as they could find but he still felt something was missing.

He heard the sound of footsteps behind him and looked around.

"Dawson," he said.

The other man nodded, looking a little worse for wear. He was wearing sunglasses despite the day being grey and overcast and his jaw was dark with stubble.

"You get called in early too?" he asked.

Jim had received the call at six that morning. Fortunately, his flatmates had gone out to a friend's place for dinner the night before and the house had been quiet, so he had managed to get an early night for a change.

"Where were you?" he asked.

The senior constable yawned. "Over at this girl's place."

"You dating?"

"Nah, met her at this bar the other night." He shrugged, "Nothing serious."

Jim tried not to let his annoyance show. Dawson had known he would be on duty that weekend so the last thing he should have been doing was going out to bars and drinking, or spending the night at a woman's place.

"So what're you looking for?" the other man asked.

Jim shook his head. "I don't really know. There was drug paraphernalia everywhere but it seems odd to me that she'd be doing drugs here in the middle of the night."

The other man shrugged again. "These kids do stupid things at times."

"Maybe. Maybe not."

"Well, I dunno. Got an i.d. on the kid anyway. Name's Lori Mattison. She's a student at Fraley."

Well, wasn't that a coincidence, Jim thought. The very school Amanda was investigating for drug dealing. He recalled the name from Amanda's daily reports.

"Seems rather a coincidence, given that other kid's death last week," he said.

Dawson sighed. "Well, we won't know anything

until we get the results back from the coroner.

Which could take days, Jim thought. Even the preliminary results would take a couple of days at least. If something bad was going on, with Amanda right smack-bang in the middle of it, he worried she might be in danger.

Still, from what he'd noted from the crime scene, this looked to be a drug overdose. Since Lori had hung out with Amanda's two chief suspects, Jim had to assume it was an accident until he heard otherwise.

Knowing at least one of the boys had seen him with Amanda, he asked another detective, Dave Campion, to bring the youths in for an interview. He watched the interviews on the monitor in the next room.

Kyle was brought in around ten. He had clearly only just got out of bed as his clothes were rumpled and he hadn't shaved.

Jim instantly disliked the teen. He could see what Amanda meant when she had said there was something about the boy. He had walked in with a kind of swagger, as if he was confident police had nothing on him and couldn't touch him.

"Kyle, thanks for coming in," Dave said, taking what Jim thought was a softly-softly approach. It wasn't the approach he would use, but then again, Dave didn't have the same information he did.

The seventeen-year-old shrugged. "Whatever."

"Did you know Lori Mattison?"

"Yeah, she hung out. My mate Jake is her cousin. Why?"

"Lori was found dead this morning. Did you know she took drugs?"

Kyle raised an eyebrow. "Her? Nah man, she never touched them."

"Are you sure about that?"

"Lori … I mean, she wasn't bad or nothing. She was all right, I guess."

"What was your relationship with her?"

"Like I said. She hung out. Her and that new girl. Mandy." He shifted on the hard wooden chair. Jim had deliberately made sure there were no comfortable chairs in the interview room. It was classic psychology, he thought. If a suspect or an interview subject was too relaxed, they were less likely to give anything away.

"Maybe that girl Mandy knows something."

Jim could see Dave storing that information away. His colleague wasn't aware of Amanda's involvement in the case.

"What about you, Kyle? Are you doing drugs these days?"

"Nah, man, I'm clean. Look, I'm sorry about the kid. Really. But it's nothing to do with me."

"Yeah, I'll bet," Jim said to himself.

The interview with Jake was the same. Annoyed, Jim reported to his boss. Pete was off-duty, but Jim had made a point of informing the sergeant what had happened.

"I just came back from seeing Amanda," his boss

told him over the phone.

"How is she doing?" Jim asked, concerned about the girl.

"She's devastated. She actually liked the girl."

"Yeah, I kind of got that from her reports. It looks like the girl wasn't as innocent as Amanda thought."

"What about the two boys?"

"Dave interviewed them but we got nothing. They pretended they had no idea Lori was doing drugs."

One thing had come out of the interviews. Neither boy had acted shocked or upset in any way. For a girl who had hung out with them on a fairly regular basis, they didn't seem to care she was dead.

"Damn! These boys are too smart for their own good," Pete replied when Jim gave him his assessment of the interviews.

"I guess I should talk to Amanda."

"She'll be on her way to the station," his boss told him. "She figured you'd need to talk to her."

"Jim?"

He looked up at Dave. "Yeah?"

"Amanda's here to see you."

Jim turned back to the phone. "Boss?"

"Yeah, I heard. Go easy on her, okay? She's had a bit of a shock today."

"Thanks. I will."

He got up from his desk and joined his colleague.

"You didn't tell me that was the boss' daughter," Dave said in a loud whisper.

"You didn't ask," he replied.

"She sure is a looker."

He looked at his co-worker. Dave was about a year or so older than him. He was taller than Jim by about five centimetres with a slightly thinner build.

Dave had just joined them about a month earlier from another station in the city. He hadn't met Amanda in person.

As they reached the door to the outer office, Dave paused a moment, straightening his tie and combing a hand through his dark blond hair. Jim cocked an eyebrow at him.

"Dude, she's not here for a social call."

"I know that," Dave replied, looking miffed.

Rolling his eyes, Jim opened the door. Amanda was sitting quietly in the waiting area, her gaze locked on the empty secretary's office. She was pale, but dry-eyed.

"Amanda?"

She looked around, frowning at Dave before biting her lip as she looked at Jim.

"Come on," Jim said kindly. "We can talk in your dad's office."

Dave nudged him. Jim sighed. "Amanda Steele, Dave Campion."

He saw a hint of a smile from Amanda at his exasperation. He was sure she would normally have said something cutting, but figured it must have been the shock she'd had that morning.

He led the way back into the office and grabbed a chair for Amanda. Dave stood in the doorway.

"Uh ..."

"Why don't you go write up your notes on the interviews," Jim suggested. "And would you mind closing the door on your way out?"

Amanda snickered softly as his colleague did as he was told. Jim waited until the door was closed before sitting down.

"How are you doing?" he asked.

"I ... honestly, I just can't believe what's happened. Do you know ..."

"It looks like an accidental overdose. We'll know more when we get the report from the coroner."

She shook her head. "I just ... I mean, Lori just didn't seem ..."

"That's a little naïve, don't you think?" he asked gently.

"I guess."

"Amanda, I hate to ask, but where were you last night?"

"I went to the bar ... the same one I went to last week. Lori turned up around eleven, or just after. I wasn't really keeping time. Anyway, Kyle bought me a beer but before I could drink it, Lori spilled it."

He frowned at her. "You let some guy buy you a beer?"

She looked at him, adopting what he assumed was supposed to be an innocent expression. His frown deepened. He was sure Amanda wasn't that naïve!

"Yeah, why?"

He shook his head. There were so many things

wrong with that scenario, but he wasn't about to ask her what she was thinking.

"Anyway, I left the bar and got a taxi home. I guess that was about eleven-thirty. I got home about twelve-fifteen, took a shower and went to bed."

"Did you notice anything unusual about Lori's behaviour?"

"She was trying to get me to leave when Kyle and her cousin showed up. She was arguing with him, but I couldn't tell what they were arguing about."

He frowned at her. "Arguing with who?"

"Jake."

He made a mental note to get Jake back in for more questioning. The youth had made no mention of any kind of argument with his cousin.

"So when you left the bar Lori was fine?"

Amanda nodded. She took a deep breath.

"Is this because of me?"

"What do you mean?"

"Do you think I did something that would make Lori …"

"Amanda, we don't know anything at this stage. It's going to take a couple of days at least to get some preliminary results. Even then we probably won't have anything conclusive."

"I just … something isn't adding up, Jim. I never saw Lori take anything."

"You've only known the girl for two weeks."

"Even so, I should have seen something. She

knew who I was pretending to be."

"How so?"

"She was saying something last night about what happened at my 'old school'. Like she knew all about it. You knew someone broke into the file. I mean, we anticipated that anyway, but …"

"Amanda, I'm sorry, but you can't assume …"

"I'm not assuming anything!"

"You're being incredibly naïve!"

"That's your opinion!"

"Oh my god, it's no wonder you failed to get into police college with that attitude!"

She glared at him. "Well, who'd want to be a cop if they're all as close-minded as you!"

"I'm not close-minded. It's called being realistic and you'd see that if you'd get your head out of the goddamn clouds. Amanda, damn it, I'm trying to help you here!"

She stood up. "Well, I don't want your help!"

Before he could stop her, she flung open the door and walked out, striding angrily back to the exit. Jim sighed heavily.

"Great! Just frickin' great!" He ran a hand through his hair. "What the hell just happened?"

Chapter Seventeen

Going back to the school the day after Lori was found dead was difficult for Amanda. It hadn't taken long for rumours to spread over the entire school. It was worse than the stories that had spread with Mitchell's death. The students would become suspiciously quiet the moment she walked into a room, as if she was guilty by association.

Kyle and Jake had not turned up at the school that morning. Amanda wasn't sure if they had taken off in order to avoid more questions from the police or if they were pretending to be so upset over Lori's death that they couldn't deal with school.

She was still upset over the quarrel with Jim. Having had a little time to think over what he'd said, she could see it from his perspective. His view was that she was being naïve, but then he hadn't spent any time with Lori. She was sure she would have known if the girl was doing drugs. There were always signs. At least, that was what she believed. A small part of her did have some doubts.

Donaldson called her into his office halfway through Monday. He sat at his desk, his head in his hands, obviously upset.

"I'm not sure we should continue this," he said. "Things are ..."

"You can't give up now," she said.

He looked at her. Amanda could tell he was stressed and worried and not just about his job.

"Two students have died in what seems to me suspicious circumstances. Both since I hired your firm to do this investigation. I just don't think it's wise ..."

She did her best to placate him, even as she wondered if he was implying she was somehow at fault. Of course that could have been her own feelings of guilt causing her to misread the situation.

"Matt, I understand. I do. You're scared. I'm worried myself, but I'm not about to let it stop me doing my job. Call me naïve or whatever, but I'm going to finish this, with or without your approval."

"Well, I don't want you getting hurt," he said, making it clear he wasn't blaming her at all but was actually worried about her.

"I don't plan on it," she replied, even knowing that this wasn't exactly something she could foresee. She wasn't psychic, after all.

He looked at her, clearly not reassured, but almost resigned. She gazed back at him with a look of determination. She was damned if she was going to just give up now when things looked bad.

Her father had already tried to talk her out of

continuing with the assignment, but she had refused to listen. What kind of cop would back down on an investigation when things started getting dangerous? she'd asked him. He'd reminded her that she wasn't a cop, but as far as she was concerned the principle was the same.

"What about the two boys Lori spent time with?"

"I'm sure one of them at least is involved in whatever's been going on. I'm not so sure it's all about drug dealing. I think there's something else, something deeper."

"How do you plan on finding that out?"

"I'm going to talk to a few kids, see if I can't get them to open up about it."

Donaldson shook his head. "I don't know. I really don't see how ..."

"Look, we both know there is a certain element in this school that act like they rule over everyone else. I'm not suggesting you pull in everyone in that group, but we have to start somewhere. Don't you have a guidance counsellor?"

He shot her an odd look before replying. "Of course we do."

"Then let's start there."

He seemed puzzled as if trying to follow Amanda's reasoning. Amanda wasn't exactly sure where she was going with the idea, but it was a place to start.

"What would you suggest?"

"Set up a meeting," she said. "Sooner the better."

He turned to his computer to check the counsellor's schedule, then turned back to her.

"She's free tomorrow morning."

"Slot me in," Amanda told him. She glanced at the clock. "Looks like school time is over."

Students were already leaving for the day when she left the office and made her way to the front gate. Amanda wasn't sure what she was hoping to see, but she studied the students' faces as they walked out.

She spotted Mitchell Cole's girlfriend walking with her head down. Emma was understandably upset over her boyfriend's death. She had spent most of the past week away from school, so it was no surprise to see the pretty redhead looking pale and grieved. She clutched books to her chest in a way that seemed to Amanda like a defensive measure.

A youth stopped the girl with a hand on her arm. She looked up through the curtain of hair and shrank back, looking almost frightened. Amanda frowned at the girl's demeanour. She pulled out her phone, pretending to be texting as she took a couple of shots of the pair.

She was half expecting Jim to call that afternoon or even that night but guessed he was probably tied up with interviews. She wrote up her report and sent it off to her boss and decided to have an early night.

The next morning at the appointed time she left

class and knocked on the guidance counsellor's door.

"Come in."

She opened the door slowly and entered the room. The counsellor looked up from the desk.

"Amanda?"

She nodded. "Yes. Mr Donaldson thought ..."

"I know," the woman replied.

Amanda glanced at the nameplate on the desk. It was just a piece of wood cut in a triangular shape with a cheap plastic plate made to look like brass stuck on the surface. On the wall was a framed certificate stating that Yvonne Tanner had graduated from Victoria University with a degree in psychology. Amanda couldn't read the date but the frame looked like it had been there a while.

"Sit down," Ms Tanner told her.

She bit her lip, gazing back at the slightly-built woman, thinking that she had to be in her late forties at least. The years had not been kind to the counsellor, whose face and neck had taken on the leathery appearance of someone who spent too much time in the sun without some sort of protection. Amanda could see the dark roots peeping through the woman's obviously dyed blonde hair. It also had the dry, damaged look of too much bleaching.

The counsellor folded her hands in front of her.

"Well, Amanda. I think I know why you're here. From your file, I see that you haven't been here very long. You were friends with ..." She picked up a file from her desk, squinting through her wire-rimmed glasses at the document. "Lori?"

Amanda nodded. "Yes."

"Such a tragic loss," the woman said, making a 'tsk' sound, obviously trying to be sympathetic but without much success. "How do you feel about that?"

Amanda shrugged. "I'm sad, but ... you know, I didn't know her that long."

Yvonne returned to leaning on the desk with her hands folded in front of her. She pursed her lips. "I see."

"Has anyone else come to talk to you?" Amanda asked, wincing inwardly. Yeah, that was subtle, she mentally berated herself.

The counsellor raised an eyebrow. It was dark and didn't fit the blonde look. It was also far too thin by what Amanda believed to be modern fashion, giving her face a harder, less attractive look.

"Excuse me?"

"Well, I mean, I was just curious. After what's happened in the last week, you'd think people would be, you know, walking around like the world had ended. I mean, two kids are dead. Don't you think that would be a huge deal? Yet they're walking around like they don't care."

The woman sniffed, practically looking down her nose at her.

"I hardly think you're qualified to judge how people are feeling ..." She looked down at a file on her desk, making it obvious that she hadn't bothered to remember who she was meant to be counselling. "… Amanda."

"I know, I know. But you'd think someone would at least show some feeling. Like Emma. You know, Mitchell Cole's girlfriend. I saw her yesterday. She looked pretty upset."

Yvonne was quiet for a few moments, her eyes narrowed as if she didn't like the way Amanda was leading the conversation.

"Well, of course she is very upset. But we're not talking about Emma. We're talking about you."

Amanda picked up on something in the woman's tone which suggested she might have an inkling of what had happened between Emma and her boyfriend.

"Has she said anything?"

"Amanda, please. Could we get back to …"

Amanda frowned, tuning out the counsellor as voices intruded from the corridor outside. The office had been placed in the main part of the school instead of the administration block. Students would walk past to get to their lockers.

The chatter increased, along with the sound of metal crashing against metal. Amanda got up from the chair and moved to the door.

"We're not finished young lady," Tanner admonished her, but she ignored the woman.

She stared in shock. Two uniformed police officers were blocking students from the lockers while two crime scene investigators wearing latex gloves were using bolt cutters to snip through the bolts securing each locker. The contents were being examined thoroughly. Anything that looked suspicious was placed in clear plastic bags.

"What the hell?" Amanda said, moving toward the lockers. She recognised Dawson as one of the cops keeping the students back. He stepped forward, putting out a hand.

"That's far enough," he said.

"What's going on?"

"This is none of your business," Dawson told her, his eyes darting to the outer door on the opposite end of the hallway. His words were clearly to keep the students still within earshot from getting curious, while his body language told her something else.

Amanda stood still for a moment, then turned and began walking back along the corridor, avoiding the rest of the student body. She opened the exit door, ignoring the shouts from the teachers who were trying to round up the students and telling them to go to the assembly hall.

A hand grabbed her wrist and pulled her away from the door, down onto the grass beside the building and out of sight of the corridor. She looked up, startled.

"Jim? What's going on? Why are you guys searching lockers?"

He shook his head. "You might have been right about Lori," he said. "Coroner came back with preliminary results this morning. She was murdered."

Chapter Eighteen

Jim could see Amanda's face turn white with shock.

"Wha ... how, who ..."

"The how is fairly obvious. The what and the who, that's another question."

"My God, Jim!"

He glanced through the doorway. Students were still milling about in the corridor. Despite what had happened, he wasn't going to risk breaking Amanda's cover. If she suddenly disappeared from the school, it could place her in more danger.

"You better get back in there," he said.

"No," she replied stubbornly.

"Amanda, listen to me. If the same people who did this to Lori figure out who you are, they could come after you. Maintain your cover for now. At least until we can assess the situation."

Amanda looked reluctant but he pushed her back in the direction of the school hall.

"Go," he said.

She shrugged and sighed, slipping back inside to join the rest of the students. He waited a few moments before following, stopping to watch the forensics team working.

The school principal was talking to Dawson, who waved him over. Jim approached them.

"What's up?"

Donaldson looked apologetic as he spoke.

"I've already had a phone call from a lawyer insisting you cease and desist."

"Sorry, but the search warrant we have overrides any cease and desist order," Jim replied. "You go back to the lawyer and tell him this is a homicide investigation and we have a warrant signed by a High Court Justice."

Donaldson swallowed visibly.

"Uh, yes, of course."

Jim pulled him aside. "Look, I get you're worried about your job and the kids here, but a girl has been murdered."

"I know, it's just ... This is getting out of hand. I hired Amanda to ..."

"I know," Jim told him. "But this is something neither you nor Amanda could have predicted or prevented. Frankly, I'm surprised it took this long for it to blow up as it has. We both know that whatever precipitated this has been going on for some time. Maybe Amanda's being here didn't help, but it would have happened eventually, with or without her."

"So what do I do?" the other man asked,

flustered. He was out of his depth and he knew it.

"Your job," Jim replied quietly. "Talk to the students. Make it clear that we're only interested in finding anything that might tell us who killed Lori. Also tell them that if they know anything, anything at all, they need to talk to us."

Donaldson walked away, clearly upset. Jim recalled the story his boss had told him about the man. What had once been a troubled teen was a man who genuinely cared about the kids under his supervision. It must hurt, Jim thought, to feel like nothing you do makes a difference after all. He didn't think that was necessarily true. Matt Donaldson could still turn this around, if he was smart and didn't cave to the demands of the parents and the school board.

His phone beeped and he pulled it out to check the message, then looked up at Dawson.

"Stay with the crew. Pathologist wants to see me."

The senior constable nodded and turned back to keeping a close watch on the team still examining the lockers.

Jim left the school and headed into town. The mortuary was in the basement of the city hospital, only reached via a maze of corridors. There were a few autopsies under way as Jim noticed teams working in various rooms. He continued along the cool corridor and knocked on a door.

"Billy."

The young pathologist looked up from his

computer and smiled at him. Jim had been friends with Billy Chang in high school but their choices of career had seen them go off in different directions once high school was over.

Billy had completed his degree, but as he still needed to complete his specialist training he was only a registrar. At school he'd been one of the high achiever students who preferred to focus more on their studies than partying. He'd once told Jim that it was considered normal in China. At least in the area his parents had grown up. There had been great emphasis on working hard and less emphasis on play.

Billy's parents had decided when they married that they would move to New Zealand, if only to give their child a better life than he would have had in China. However, the work habits passed down through the generations had been difficult for them to shake.

Jim hadn't been surprised to learn his old friend was working at the hospital.

"Hey Jim. Long time no see."

"Yeah, I know. I meant to call you when I transferred up here, but it's been rather busy. So what've you got for me?"

"Okay, the results aren't confirmed yet, but I'm pretty sure the victim was subdued before she was killed. We found what looks like cotton fibres in her nose and throat. They're still testing the fibres, so I can't say it's a hundred percent."

Jim nodded. Forensic tests would take days. More in-depth analysis would take weeks to be completed. Even then, they wouldn't be conclusive.

"So she was smothered?" he asked.

"Until she passed out? Yes. I believe so."

The call earlier that morning that had prompted the search at the school had confirmed Lori Mattison's death as a drug overdose. However, toxicology screening had also shown that the girl had never touched drugs in her life, other than prescription or over-the-counter drugs, he assumed. Kyle at least hadn't been lying about that."

"What else?" he asked his friend.

"Some bruising. There was a large bruise on her wrist which indicates to me someone grabbed her wrist hard enough to almost break the bone."

"Is there anything to tell us whether only one guy was involved?"

Billy shook his head. "The results are inconclusive. We swabbed for DNA, but we won't get the results back from the lab for a few weeks."

Jim knew that would happen. If he was going to catch the killer, he was going to have to rely on good old-fashioned investigating rather than evidence.

"There is one other thing," the pathologist told him. "What we found in her system wasn't just one single drug. It was a combination of them."

"Like what?"

"Ecstasy, methamphetamine, GHB."

"GHB?" he asked, something nagging the back of his mind.

"Gamma-hydroxybutyrate," his friend replied.

Jim shook his head. "I know what it is. It's a date-rape drug."

"One of many," Billy returned. He went on to explain that while there had been drug paraphernalia scattered around the crime scene, it all seemed to have been set up to look like the girl had been taking drugs alone. Except for a syringe which had traces of her blood on it, none of it could be conclusively traced to her.

He also told Jim that Lori had died probably within minutes of the drugs entering her bloodstream, which was why they hadn't had time to metabolise. GHB usually disappeared within a few hours, provided the victim was alive.

As he left the hospital, Jim couldn't shake off a nagging feeling that he was missing something important but just couldn't put his finger on what it was.

Back at the station, he headed upstairs to the bullpen, only to be confronted by a hysterical woman. She was in her late forties with greying brown hair. He stared at her as she screamed at him, demanding to know what he was going to do about the situation. He glanced at Kerry, who was sitting in her office, clearly trying to keep well out of it.

"Ma'am," he said. "You need to calm down."

"Don't you tell me to calm down. I want to know what you're going to do about this."

He stared at her, completely confused, regretting his choice of entering the building through the front rather than from the back of the station.

"About what, ma'am? I don't even know who you are."

An older man stepped into view. He was wearing the standard police uniform. There were three silver pips on his lapel indicating his rank of inspector. The woman turned to look at him.

"Mrs Mattison," he said. "Perhaps you'd like to step into my office and calm yourself."

Jim frowned at the older officer. Mark Gerraghty held the most senior rank at the station of Area Commander. His role was mostly administrative, but it was a position he had earned after more than twenty years on the job.

Gerraghty gently guided the woman toward his office before turning to look back at Jim.

"She's been here for the last hour, screaming about her daughter. Want to tell me what's been going on?"

"Her daughter is the victim of a homicide sir," Jim told his commander. "It was only just confirmed through preliminary results this morning. I hadn't got around to writing up my report."

"I see," the older man replied, scratching his upper lip. "What would you prefer I tell this woman?"

Jim wanted to tell his boss that it really wasn't his place to do so, but decided it was safer not to comment.

"Please tell her that we will do our best to find out who murdered her daughter sir."

Gerraghty nodded. "Yes, that's all we can do. Tell Pete I'd like to talk to him once I'm through with Mrs Mattison."

"Yes sir," Jim replied,

He entered the CIB area and headed immediately to Pete's office. He was surprised to see Amanda sitting in the chair opposite her father. She looked upset.

"Amanda, honey, this is not your fault."

"Tell that to Lori," the girl responded morosely.

Pete looked up. "Hey Jim. So what have you got?"

Jim hesitated, glancing uneasily at the blonde.

"Uh, maybe it's better if you read the report, sir," he said.

Amanda glared at him. "Don't you dare!" she said. "This is my case and you are not keeping me out of the loop."

"Amanda, sweetheart, I hate to say this, but I think it's time you withdraw from the case. This is a murder investigation now."

"But Dad ..."

Jim bit his lip. While he could understand Amanda's need to finish what she had started, he agreed with her father.

"We'll discuss this later," Pete told his daughter. "Go home and change out of that uniform."

Jim noticed for the first time Amanda was still wearing the uniform from the school. It was obvious she hadn't stopped at work to change her clothes before heading to the station. That hadn't exactly been smart, he thought.

Amanda looked sullen, but got up.

"I'll walk you out," Jim told her. She walked past him out the door, then looked back at him expectantly. He turned back to his boss.

"Uh, the boss wants to see you."

His boss nodded. "Thanks. I'll be right out."

Jim walked beside Amanda, making sure to keep pace with her.

"Are you okay?" he asked.

"No."

"Look, Amanda, I ..."

He really didn't know what to say to her. This was her first case and she'd got in over her head. Not that she really needed him to tell her that.

He opened the door, only to find Lori's mother walking out of the office at the same time. She spotted Amanda in uniform.

"You!" she said, pointing a chubby finger at Amanda. "I bet you're one of those troublemakers at that school. God, I knew I should have pulled her out of there!" She placed her hands on wide hips and glared at Amanda through beady eyes. The woman was massively obese, with a thin mouth above triple chins. She wore a pearl necklace which seemed to randomly disappear in the layers of fat.

Jim was reminded of a famous male actor who had worn a fat suit and dressed in drag for a movie.

The mother looked like a caricature of that character. It would have been laughable if she hadn't looked so scary. Jim could see tracks of mascara down her cheeks. She'd clearly been crying.

Amanda looked taken aback as the woman stared at her as if she could set her on fire with a look.

"You and those boys, stirring up trouble at that school. My Lori was a good girl. You did it, didn't you? My daughter's dead because of you!"

Amanda's face showed a myriad of emotions as she stared at the belligerent and grieving woman. Jim reached out a hand to try to stop her when she turned away but she was already moving, running down the stairs as if the devil was after her.

Chapter Nineteen

"It's your fault!"

The words played over and over in her head as Amanda tossed and turned the next day. She had already spent an entire night unable to sleep for hearing them again and again.

Her phone had rung beside the bed several times that morning and a few times the night before. Two calls were from her boss, Moody. Jim had called at least four times, while her father had called probably about half a dozen. She had ignored every one.

"It is my fault," she told herself as she lay staring up at the ceiling in the dim light of day. "I got her killed."

It hurt. It wasn't just the murder. It was the fact that she had failed in her job.

It was little wonder that she had been rejected from police college. She was hopeless. She was a lousy investigator.

"You're an idiot," she said into the empty room, not for the first time.

She had heard Penny leave for work hours earlier. Amanda hadn't bothered to tell her flatmate what had happened. Even if Penny knew what had really been going on, Amanda doubted she would understand. There were times when she thought the woman lived on a different planet than everyone else.

She rolled over and punched her pillow, exhaustion finally overriding the voices in her head and quieting them enough for her to sleep.

She woke when her bedroom door hit the wall. Blinking sleep out of her eyes, she sat up. Penny stood in the doorway, hands on her hips.

"Why the hell don't you answer your phone?" she scolded crossly.

"Go away!" she muttered while picking up her pillow and covering her face with it, really not in the mood to deal with the woman.

"I can't. Your boyfriend's here. He's been trying to call you all day."

Penny pulled at the blankets.

"Are you seriously telling me you've been sleeping all day?" she asked, her voice rising a couple of octaves so it sounded almost like a screeching owl. "Get out of bed and talk to your boyfriend."

"He is not my boyfriend!" Amanda returned, sitting up to glare at her flatmate. Penny's eyebrows shot up.

"Oh, really? So you wouldn't mind if I asked him out sometime?"

Amanda rolled her eyes, then waved her hand.

"Do what you want. It's a free country."

Jim appeared in the doorway.

"Amanda? Why don't you answer your phone? Your dad's been calling ... I've been calling ..."

She flopped back down on the mattress.

"Damn it, don't you get the message? Leave me alone!"

"No. Amanda we need to talk about what happened yesterday."

She propped herself up on her elbows.

"I don't need to talk to <u>you</u> about anything," she said.

"Does that also apply to your father? He's worried about you. Look, if it's about what that woman said, she's wrong! This isn't your fault!"

"She's right! I got her killed!"

Penny stared at her. "Got who killed?" she asked.

"None of your business!" Amanda snapped.

Realising she wasn't going to get rid of Jim that easily, she got out of bed and pushed past him to leave the room. He followed her as she entered the bathroom.

"Amanda ..."

She stared at him. "God, can't you even let a girl pee in peace? Get out!"

To his credit, he looked a little embarrassed.

"Uh, geeze. Sorry." He backed out and she closed the door.

"We really do need to talk about this," he said through the closed door.

"I don't want to talk. I want to be left alone."

"I can't do that."

Penny seemed to be trying to score points with Jim by suggesting making coffee for them so that they'd all calm down. Amanda flushed the toilet and listened to her flatmate chatter away to the detective as she washed her hands. Jim was replying with monosyllabic answers.

She stared at her reflection in the bathroom mirror. Her face was pale and the little bit of make-up she'd worn the day before had smudged around her eyes, giving her the 'panda-eye' look and emphasising the lack of colour in her cheeks. She grabbed a washcloth and rinsed it under warm water, washing the make-up off her face. When she was done, she checked her reflection again. She was still pale, but at least the smudged make-up was gone.

She could hear Penny still chattering away. Her name was mentioned but Amanda couldn't make out what was being said. The sound of her flatmate's voice was irritating, making her feel almost trapped. Penny was probably trying to wheedle information out of Jim and the last thing Amanda wanted was to be around when she was the subject of the conversation.

"God, I need to get out of here," she muttered.

She opened the door a crack and glanced toward the living room. Jim was sitting on the couch with a coffee mug in his hands. The older woman sat beside him, still trying to talk to him.

Amanda rolled her eyes and returned to her bedroom. She opened her wardrobe door and stared at the contents, then grabbed a pair of jeans and a halter top before also grabbing her favourite pair of leather boots. They came up to shin height on her and had a scroll design on the side, reminding her a little of cowboy boots. They had a low block heel which she had liked as they were comfortable for walking along the city streets. She dressed quickly, then brushed her long blonde hair.

Jim stood up when she emerged from her room.

"Where are you going?" he asked as she grabbed her jacket from the coat stand. It was brown suede, with fringes along the sleeves.

"Out," she said. "And don't follow me."

"Damn it, Amanda. Don't be stupid!"

She turned and sent him a frosty glare.

"So now I'm stupid? Good to know."

She didn't miss the way her flatmate put a proprietary hand on the man's arm. She snorted. They were welcome to each other.

She hadn't made any kind of plan other than to just get away from the house. The trouble was, she thought, this was the kind of problem she couldn't run away from.

It was already dark by the time she drove into town. Still without any idea of what to do, she decided to park the car in a side street and walk around for a while.

A cold wind blew up from the harbour and she pulled at the edges of her jacket, as if that could keep the breeze from passing through the suede fabric.

Other people were also walking the streets, most likely going for dinner at a restaurant. There were couples dressed up in what Amanda remembered her grandmother had called her 'Sunday best'. Her maternal grandmother lived further south, preferring small-town life to that in the 'big smoke', unlike her son-in-law, she would often lament.

Her grandmother Elise had been born in the 'baby boom,' the nickname given to the post-war era when there had been a temporary increase in the birth rate due to the return of soldiers from overseas. While she had been a teenager long after fashions had dictated women dressed more casually in everyday life, some of those in her generation still dressed up for social occasions.

Amanda continued walking, wrapping her arms around herself to keep warm and ignoring the strange looks from others passing by. Despite the fact most retail shops in the street were closed, the inner city was still a bustling hive of activity. Many of the fast-food restaurants were still crowded with diners and a couple of buskers were singing or playing to crowds.

A small group were gathered on one side of the footpath, seeking shelter from the cold wind by huddling under store canopies or awnings. Amanda could smell the distinct odour of unwashed bodies along with tobacco and something else. She ducked her head and tried to avoid eye contact.

It wasn't that she didn't feel sympathy for the homeless, but she just wished they wouldn't crowd the city streets. She had known of a girl who refused to walk alone because she was afraid she might be accosted by someone trying to get money for food. She had been led to believe that most of them wasted the money they did get on alcohol and cigarettes.

"Hey, you got any money?"

Amanda froze mid-step, refusing to lift her head. The man who had stepped in front of her literally stunk from head to toe. If it wasn't the stench of stale sweat, it was the smell of his breath. She could have become intoxicated on the fumes alone.

"You got any money?" he repeated.

She shook her head and tried to duck around the man, but he refused to get out of her way.

"Hey, I'm talking to you."

"Leave me alone," she said quietly.

"I said you got any money? I gotta eat." He swayed. Amanda wasn't sure what he'd drunk but it smelled suspiciously like methylated spirits, which was pure alcohol with some nasty additives. She had heard that some drank that instead of diluted alcohol because their tolerance was such that they no longer got a buzz from it.

"Leave me alone!" she said more forcefully.

He grabbed her arm. Amanda began to feel light-headed. She pulled away, feeling something tear from the sleeve and kicked him in the shin, hard enough to incapacitate him temporarily. He yelled as she shoved him away and began to run, glad she had chosen to wear her boots as they were hard enough to bruise someone if she kicked them and low enough that she could run without fear of hurting her feet.

When she finally stopped running, she looked around, realising it was too dark for her to see where she was. Amanda had spent her childhood exploring the city, but this was at night in an area that was neglected by the council. Most of the street lights weren't working.

She began walking at a hurried pace; seeing shadows in doorways as she looked around in the hope that she might spot something familiar. Her heart was pounding as she kept walking; wanting to be anywhere else but where she was.

Something grabbed the sleeve of her jacket and she screamed.

"Whoa, hey, I'm sorry babe."

She turned and peered at the man. She could barely see his face.

"I didn't mean to scare you," he said. "You just looked a little lost."

"Uh, yeah. I guess I got turned around."

She shivered as the wind blasted through her once more.

"You're freezing," he said. He had an accent that reminded her of her cousin, who had grown up in Australia. "Come on. Let's get you someplace warm."

"Uh, thanks. I'm all right. Maybe I should just go find my car and go home." She shivered again. The man sounded sympathetic as he spoke.

"You spend any more time out here and you'll freeze your butt off," he told her. "Come on. I promise I'm not an axe murderer."

She heard the cajoling tone and was forced to laugh. He sounded a little like Jim, when the detective was actually being friendly.

She let the man lead her down the darkened street. Her head was telling her this was not a good situation, but she figured she could always ditch him as soon as she got her bearings.

She was relieved a few minutes later when they turned into a well-lit street. She still wasn't sure where she was exactly but the lighting told her that it was at least reasonably well-populated.

She got a good look at her 'rescuer'. He was well-built and tall, although not nearly as tall as Jim, she decided. He had a handsome face which was slightly marred by a scar which stretched over half his face under his eye. A lock of dirty blond hair fell over his other eye, giving him a sort of rakish look.

"Where did you get that scar?" she asked.

He grinned. "Rescuing a damsel in distress," he replied, eliciting another laugh from her. He guided her with a gentle hand on her elbow. "Come on. It's just down here."

Amanda followed him down an alley to what seemed to be a small bar. She glanced up at the sign. The Celtic Inn.

As he opened the door, she peeked inside the dimly lit bar. It was everything she figured an inn would be. A bar with polished wood was along the far wall. The bartender was a tall man with what looked like a Celtic tattoo on his arm.

There were four booths with benches padded with velvet-covered cushions and tables scattered around the main floor. All but one of the tables were full and two of the booths were empty.

The man led her to a booth and waited for her to sit down before sitting opposite her. Behind him, Amanda could see a roaring fire. She closed her eyes, loving the warmth as it slowly thawed the chill in her body.

"You got a name?" he asked. "I usually like to know the names of girls I rescue."

"Amanda."

"DJ," he said. "Well, actually it's Dominic Joseph, but my friends all call me DJ." He leaned forward, his elbows on the table. Amanda frowned slightly, thinking once again of her Gran who thought elbows on the table was the height of rudeness when dining out.

"So, Amanda. What brings a girl like you out on a cold night?"

She shrugged. "Just … you know, thinking."

He smiled. "And what could a pretty girl like you have to think about? You should have the world at your feet."

She shook her head. "I screwed up. Badly."

He frowned in sympathy. "Want to talk about it?"

"No," she said.

"Can I get you anything?" a voice asked. Amanda looked up, staring at the woman, who was gazing back at them with an enquiring look. She had a notepad in her hand. Amanda frowned, used to bars where customers bought their drinks at the bar before sitting at a table.

"Um …"

DJ smiled again at her. "What you need is to forget all about your troubles. At least for one night." He looked up at the woman. "Whiskey," he said, ordering one for each of them.

Amanda shook her head. She'd never drunk any kind of spirits other than the occasional RTD and wasn't about to start now.

"Trust me," he said. "This will take the edge off."

"No, I can't," she replied.

"Trust me," he repeated.

She bit her lip, wondering what kind of trouble she had got herself into. The waitress walked off.

"I didn't know this place existed," Amanda replied. "And I grew up here."

"The owner happens to be a friend of mine," DJ told her.

Amanda took her jacket off, noticing as she did so there was a slight rip in the fabric. It must have been when the drunk had grabbed her, she thought, frowning. Damn. Still, there wasn't much she could do about it.

She sat back and listened to the music playing. The bar was unusual in that it wasn't loud rock music playing but instrumental music with soft rhythm. It was soothing.

The waitress returned with their drinks. Amanda stared at the amber liquid in the tumbler.

"I've never had whiskey before," she told DJ.

"Ahh, virgin in the house," he announced. She felt herself blushing. He chuckled. "Here's your first lesson. Whiskey, also known as bourbon, or scotch, especially your first taste of it, should be savoured. Trust me, you'll want to sip it, not scull it."

She frowned at him. "Why?"

"Because it's a very strong spirit. If it's been distilled correctly, that is. My friend doesn't water down the stuff like most bars do. Try it."

Biting her lip, Amanda hesitated, but the encouraging smile from her companion had her figuring one drink couldn't hurt.

She lifted the glass and took a sip and was glad she did. The liquid burned her throat, making her cough and her eyes water. For a moment she thought she was going to throw up as it made its way down. Unlike the vodka mix she was used to drinking, this was very strong-tasting. Strong enough to numb her taste buds, she thought.

A girl not used to hard drinking could get drunk very quickly on this stuff, she thought.

Chapter Twenty

"Where is she?" Jim could hear the worry in his boss' tone.

"I don't know boss. She left the flat a couple of hours ago."

It had taken him at least half an hour to get away from Amanda's place. Her flatmate only wanted to talk about herself and was clearly trying to flirt with him. She obviously didn't give a damn about Amanda and how she was feeling.

Worried about Amanda's state of mind, Jim had gone looking for her. He understood how she felt after that horrible woman had acted but running away wasn't going to help. Especially when she hadn't taken her phone.

After an hour of searching the local area, he knew he would have to bite the bullet and called her father, asking him for the locations of Amanda's usual haunts.

He drove along the motorway toward the inner city, frowning as he spotted a police car on the other side of the highway parked behind a familiar-looking vehicle. He sped up and drove to the nearest exit, the called Central Communications. The operator quickly tracked the number of the police car and patched him through. Jim told the officer to stall the driver until he could get there.

It still took him ten minutes to get there as he'd had to cross the motorway overbridge to get to the nearest exit behind them. The two officers looked around as he pulled up his car behind the police car. Two young guys were in the backseat. Judging from the way they were sitting awkwardly their hands had been cuffed behind them.

"You'll never guess who the car belongs to," one of the officers told him gleefully. Jim nodded. The car was nothing fancy, just a small Yaris that was around fifteen years old, but Amanda's father had told him that she'd bought the car herself with money she'd earned working part-time after school.

"Yeah, I know," Jim told him. "It's Pete Steele's daughter. What about these two?"

"We caught them joyriding. Well, actually, a passing motorist called it in when they spotted the guys weaving all over the show. We breathalysed the driver."

The officer went on to explain the youth had been over four times the legal limit.

Jim crouched down beside the car and spoke to the pair. "Want to tell me where you found the car?" he asked.

"We didn't find nothing," one of the youths replied.

"Yeah, we didn't ..."

"Shut up and listen very carefully. You're already in a hell of a lot of trouble but if you help me out here I might be able to help you out a little."

He heard the officer standing behind him mutter an 'eh?' but he didn't care.

"Now the girl who owns that car is going to be very upset to find out that you two idiots thought it would be fun to steal it and risk wrapping it around the nearest power pole. The owner happens to be a friend of mine and she's having a hard time. So do me a favour and tell me where you found it."

"High Street," the youth replied. "It was just parked there."

Jim nodded and straightened up, moving away from the car.

"Idiots," he growled.

"Everything okay?" one of the officers asked.

He shook his head. "No. But I'll take care of it. You get those two in for booking and call the tow company. Pete will take care of the towing fee."

He said nothing about Amanda being missing, knowing the word would spread like wildfire. The officers had enough to do without going out looking for a girl who should know better.

He decided to start at High Street and left his car in a parking area, knowing it was a risky proposition for opportunistic thieves. He was reminded of the first two years of his career which he'd spent patrolling the streets on foot as he walked, trying to figure out where Amanda might have gone.

There were a few homeless people milling about but Jim decided it was pointless asking them if they'd seen the blonde. He did talk to a couple of them but they either had no idea or just didn't want to get involved.

By midnight, he had begun to give it up as hopeless. He'd searched just about every bar he'd come across, to no avail. His phone rang and he glanced at the screen.

"Boss?"

"Jim. Have you found her?"

"Not yet, sir."

"It's been six hours. I'm worried."

"Yeah, me too," he said as he continued walking. He passed a group of young women wearing dresses with short skirts and high heels. They smiled at him flirtatiously but he ignored them. He spotted the sign for a bar infamous for various problems with its patrons.

"I'm just going to check this next bar. I'll call you if I find anything."

The bar was dim as he walked in. A thumping bass vibrated through the floor and music, if it could be called that, could be heard through the loudspeakers. Jim liked a lot of music, but he'd never been particularly fond of music which consisted mostly of bass and little to no rhythm.

He approached the bar, looking around but unable to see in the darkness of the dance floor where at least thirty people were gyrating, most of them badly, to the beat.

Like all the other bars he'd checked tonight, he decided it wasn't wise to show his identification. Bartenders tended to get a bit antsy when cops showed up.

He managed to worm his way through the crowd of people at the bar, his ears ringing from the loud music combined with the voices of people talking in the din and sounding more like a gaggle of geese than human beings.

"What can I get you?" the bartender, a woman about his age asked. She had sandy blonde hair pulled back in a tight ponytail. She had a horseshoe in her septum and a ring in her eyebrow.

"I'm looking for a girl," he tried, hoping the woman heard him.

"Aren't we all?" she replied with a conspiratorial smirk.

"She's a friend. About yea high," he said, holding his hand about chest level. "Blonde, pretty. Young."

"Underage?" the woman asked, immediately suspicious.

"No," he told her, shaking his head. "She's nineteen."

The bartender beckoned to the end of the bar around the corner and Jim made his way through the crowd. There was a gap where those working at the bar could slip out so they could collect any glasses from the tables.

"Are you a cop?" she asked when he finally managed to get close to her.

"Yes," he admitted, "but this girl is a friend."

The woman studied him for a moment, canting her head and looking at him dubiously as if she was debating whether to co-operate with him or not. He looked at her with a fairly neutral expression, trying to convey that he really wasn't interested in anything else going on.

"Look, we get a lot of kids in here. The bouncers check if they're legal, but hell if I know from one to the other if they're under age or not. We always check i.d. if we're not sure, but ..."

"I'm not here to bust anyone, I promise," he assured her. "We're just worried about her."

"Anything more you can give me other than blonde and pretty?" the bartender asked.

Jim remembered he had a photo of her on his phone. Amanda hadn't known he had taken it when he'd met her at the Arts Centre. He took his phone from his pocket and showed it to her.

"Yeah, she's here. I mean, I haven't seen her leave. Not that that means much. She's pretty drunk though. I refused to serve her."

"Thanks," he said.

"Hope she's not in trouble," the woman replied.

"Yeah, me too," he murmured, scanning the dance floor. It was still too dark to make out much but as he continued to scan, he spotted a blonde head in the crowd.

He thanked the woman before beginning to weave his way through the dancers and trying to find the blonde he'd just seen. He reached the spot and realised it wasn't her. A girl who he would have guessed was barely seventeen, although with the thick make-up she had practically painted on she looked older, tried to get him to dance with her. He ignored her, much to her annoyance and continued looking around.

There was a couple kissing near the loudspeaker. The woman had her back to him, but her hair was the same blonde colour as Amanda's and she looked to be about the right build. Jim managed to circle so he could get a look at the woman's face.

Damn it, he thought, grabbing her arm and pulling her away from the guy who practically had his tongue down her throat.

Amanda glared at him.

"What are you doing?"

"Saving you from making a total ass of yourself."

The man she'd been kissing shoved him.

"Hey, get your own," he said, lurching drunkenly. Jim could just see a scar on one side of the man's face.

Jim had no choice but to pull his i.d.

"Beat it, jerk! Before I arrest you for drunk and disorderly."

Amanda struggled in his grip as he began to pull her off the dance floor.

"Leave me alone! I'm not going anywhere with you."

"Oh yes you are," he told her firmly.

"You don't tell me what to do," she said petulantly.

"Well I'm not about to let you give it up to the first guy available."

As they left the bar, she stopped struggling and wrapped her arms around his neck. He stumbled as her weight pushed him slightly off balance.

"So I should give it up to you instead?" she asked, clearly trying to sound seductive.

Nek minnit, he thought as she pressed cool lips to his. Her breath smelled sour from the alcohol she'd imbibed but suddenly he didn't care. She was a beautiful young woman and she was offering.

The kiss was halted as quickly as it started. Jim glanced at her, then realised why as she staggered. She was so drunk she was on the verge of passing out. As he began to manoeuvre her into a better position in his arms so he could carry her, he decided it was not going to be an easy task. Amanda was slender but not exactly light.

She moaned and muttered something not quite loud enough that he could understand it. Jim wrapped an arm around her waist, hoping his own movement would propel her into moving. She staggered against him, mumbling something he couldn't understand. Jim shifted his weight, moving forward with great difficulty. He'd been drunk before, but never as drunk as he imagined Amanda was. It was a long walk to the car, made even more difficult with the half-conscious girl by his side.

He managed to get her to the car and put her in before getting in the other side. She was leaning with her head against the window. Sighing, Jim leaned over and buckled her seat belt then did the same with his own before starting the car and pulling out.

He debated whether to drive her straight home. He didn't want to leave her in the state she was in. Especially given her flatmate's uncaring attitude. If she was so drunk she was passing out, she could throw up and choke on her own vomit. Not exactly a pleasant proposition, he thought. He had attended a couple of cases of sudden death in his first few years as a uniformed constable and both of them had been teenagers who had drunk too much alcohol. One of them had done exactly as Jim feared Amanda would do.

The safest thing to do, he reasoned, was to take her back to his place and keep an eye on her overnight.

Amanda was clearly only semi-conscious but at least not fully unconscious. He glanced at her now and again on the thirty-minute drive to the house, listening out for any subtle changes in her breathing. Of all the stupid things she could have done, he thought, mentally berating her for her idiocy. He understood she was coming to terms with what had happened, but getting drunk off her face was not the answer. It had been downright dangerous.

As concerned as he was for her, he was just as angry at her foolishness. He'd thought Amanda was smart.

"She is smart," his boss assured him when he phoned to tell Amanda's father what he'd found.

"Really? I don't think what she's done is very smart at all," he said.

"Perhaps, but this is less to do with intelligence and more to do with her immaturity. Even I can admit my daughter is still very much a child but it's not all her fault, Jim."

"How do you mean?"

"Amanda doesn't remember, but her mother is an alcoholic. She also had a gambling addiction, but ..."

Jim wanted to disagree with his boss. Amanda had made her own choice to deal with the issue by getting completely trolleyed. Still, he could see his boss' point. Her mother's alcoholism could influence Amanda's own behaviour.

"Kim left when Amanda was eight," Peter began to explain, without being prompted. "I was working all the time and I guess I tried to deny she had a problem."

"So what happened?"

"She decided one afternoon to drive to the local pub where she proceeded to drink enough that would cause a grown man to pass out, spending every cent we had on the poky machine. Meanwhile, she'd left Amanda in the car alone for six hours. If it hadn't been winter ..."

Jim could imagine it. If it had been hot, Amanda would have most likely suffocated, if she hadn't had the sense to get out of the car.

Pete went on to tell him that a colleague had recognised the car, checked it out and found Amanda asleep in the back. The constable had gone in to the pub, found Kim and alerted Pete to the situation. The ensuing fight had ended with Kim packing her bags and leaving.

"Does Amanda know about this?" he asked.

"No. Thankfully, she's blocked most of it out. All she knows is that her mother had some health problems."

Pete had clearly never told his daughter the truth about her mother. Jim didn't think that was the wisest decision, but his boss was obviously very protective of Amanda.

He heard the sounds of movement from the bedroom and went in, just in time to see Amanda hanging over the side of the bed, about to throw up. He grabbed the bucket and shoved it under her.

"What's that?" Pete asked.

"Amanda. She's throwing up."

"Well, I'll leave you to it," his boss replied. "Make sure she drinks some water."

"Yeah, I know," Jim told him.

"And Jim? Thanks for going after her."

"No worries," he replied.

He hung up the phone and watched as Amanda retched before passing out again. He cleaned her up as best he could before finally falling into bed with an exhausted sigh.

Chapter Twenty-One

Amanda groaned as the bright light filtered through her sleep-crusted eyes. Her head was pounding as if it had split in two. She tried sitting up but fell back once more against the pillows, her body feeling as if she had run a marathon. She pulled the sheet up over her head and rolled away from the light, only for her hand to collide with something hard and unyielding.

She frowned. Her own bed in her room wasn't next to a wall and there was nothing for her to hit. She thrust her hand out again to once more hit whatever it was.

"Ow!"

She cracked her eyes open and stared in shock at the naked back of the man lying in the bed next to her. She sat up abruptly but the sudden movement caused more pounding in her head and nausea to bubble up. She fought the sensation and turned to look at her bedmate, wondering how she was going to get out of this mess she was in.

"Uh ..." she said.

The man rolled over. She was relieved to discover it was Jim, but mortified at the same time.

"Well, you're awake," he said mildly.

"Um ..."

She risked a glance under the sheet and found she was wearing just her underwear. Jim smirked at her.

"You don't remember do you?" he said.

"Remember what?" she replied.

"The earth moving. It was amazing, it was mind-blowing. You, my dear, are incredible in the sack."

She stared at him in horror. She barely tolerated the man and she'd apparently slept with him? Amanda couldn't remember anything beyond going into a few bars last night, yet according to him, they'd had ... this could not be happening.

She lay back, one hand on her forehead, groaning. Jim leaned over her.

"Relax, sweetheart. Nothing happened. Trust me, if it had, you'd know."

"Ego much?" she asked, shoving him.

He was laughing at her. She scowled.

"Is all this one big joke to you?"

He rolled his eyes and got out of bed. She was relieved to see he was wearing boxer shorts as he stood up.

She winced as he turned and glared at her. His mood had very swiftly changed from joking to furious.

"What you did last night was no joke! You were damned lucky I found you when I did, you were so trashed."

She moaned, clutching her head as the volume of his voice increased with the vehemence in his tone. It reverberated in her already aching head, creating a percussion which intensified the pounding.

"Ahh, don't yell!"

He didn't seem to care as he yelled at her.

"Have you any idea the kind of trouble you could have gotten yourself into? When I found you, you were sucking face with some guy who was clearly only interested in one thing. I had to haul your ass out of there before you ended up dead in the gutter!"

Amanda shoved the blankets back while fighting down the nausea. She felt panic rise up along with the bile when she couldn't swallow at first. Her throat felt like someone had rubbed it raw with sandpaper.

Jim was once more yelling, but she could barely understand him through the waves of dizziness and nausea. Not to mention the roaring in her ears, she thought. She ran out of the bedroom knowing she was fighting a losing battle. She realized to her consternation that she had no idea where the bathroom was. She didn't want to hear another rant from Jim so she looked around and grabbed the handle of the nearest door. It didn't budge.

She was now practically hyperventilating, one hand over her mouth as if that would stop her from throwing up everywhere. A hand grabbed her by the elbow and pulled her not-so-gently in the opposite direction past the bedroom door to another door. She was then unceremoniously shoved into the bathroom. Amanda barely made it to the toilet before she began heaving. Her stomach felt like it was being pulled inside out as she draped herself over the bowl.

She had no idea what came up, refusing to even look at the contents while pressing her feverish forehead to the cool porcelain.

She began to grow aware of her surroundings as the nausea settled and the pounding in her head slowed. She could feel the coolness of the ceramic tiles beneath her bare legs.

A face cloth was thrust in front of her and she took it, wiping her mouth, then her face.

"You're shivering."

Frowning, she realised he was right. It wasn't exactly warm sitting on the cold floor, despite the feverish heat of her body. Since she'd never been hungover before, she had no idea if that was supposed to happen. All she knew was that she didn't like the sensation.

"Come on, get up. You need coffee."

Jim's tone was harsh, which she supposed she could understand, even if she didn't really remember how she came to be in his house. She blinked up at him, still trying to make sense of it all.

He threw something at her.

"Hurry up," he said, sounding impatient.

She looked at whatever it was and realised it was a t-shirt. One of his, she assumed.

She put the shirt on over her underwear and struggled to her feet. Her head swam and she reached out, grabbing the nearest object. Thankfully it was the vanity.

"You're lucky my flatmates aren't here," he told her as she joined him in the hallway.

She nodded, padding along softly behind him as he walked along the carpeted hallway and opened a door at the end. She saw they were in a large open-plan living and dining area. An island with a marble counter separated the kitchen from the rest of the space.

Jim stood at the counter pouring coffee from a pot into two mugs. He thrust one of the mugs at her.

"I don't drink black coffee," she said.

"It's either that or water," he replied. "You're hungover."

"I know that!" she snapped, regretting it the instant it came out for the way it once more set off the pounding in her head. She winced and pressed a hand to her forehead.

"Hurts?" Jim asked. She looked at him without replying. "Good," he added.

She bit her lip. Jim appeared to be gearing up for yet another rant and she wasn't in the mood. It looked like she was going to get one regardless.

"Of all the things you could have done last night, this is by far the stupidest."

She wanted to tell him that she hadn't meant to get that drunk, but one drink had led to another and another. She couldn't remember exactly how much she'd had but it was irrelevant.

"I didn't mean …"

"You know, I knew I would regret getting involved with this! I knew you wouldn't be able to handle this."

She glared at him. She hated 'I told you sos'.

"Yeah? And what makes you the expert?"

"Aside from the fact that I've gone through months of training, not to mention five years of actually working in the field? Why the hell your boss even decided to let you attempt to work on this is beyond me. You have no idea what you're doing!"

"I know what I'm doing," she returned.

He scoffed at her.

"Right. You call that knowing what you're doing? Your stupidity last night could have got you killed! You're so goddamn full of yourself."

She didn't think that was necessarily true.

"You know, I understand why they turned you down for police college. You're a child! You wouldn't have lasted a week in training with this kind of immature bullshit!"

"So, you're telling me you've never gone out and gotten drunk?" she accused.

"That's not the bloody point!" he told her. "Do you know what it would have done to your dad if something had happened to you last night? Are you that selfish, that stupid to think you can just do whatever you please and it not affect anyone?"

"Don't call me stupid!" she yelled, wanting to hit back at him but barely able to even think of a comeback. The fire of humiliation burned her cheeks. She could barely even look at the man as he continued to berate her, wanting to be anywhere but where she was. Now she understood what was meant by wanting a hole to open up in the floor and swallow her.

A door slammed and she looked up, startled to see a young couple watching them. Jim stopped mid-rant.

"What's going on?" the woman asked, looking pointedly at Amanda.

She didn't wait to hear Jim's response, turning and walking back along the hallway. She entered the bedroom and quickly found her clothes, stripping off Jim's t-shirt before putting her jeans and blouse on and grabbing her jacket. Her keys were, thankfully, still in her jacket pocket.

She heard voices murmuring as she returned to the kitchen. They were clearly talking about her. Amanda bit her lip and looked around for the door, her eyes pointedly looking everywhere but at Jim.

A hand on her wrist stopped her before she could open the front door.

"Let me drive you home," he said quietly.

She shook her head.

"Don't do me any favours," she replied. "Besides, I'd rather walk. The air will probably help the hangover."

Amanda didn't cry easily. She liked to think she was made of tougher stuff than that. Yet, as she began walking away from the house, the tears fell unbidden.

It hurt to admit it, but Jim was right. About everything. The problem was, she had no idea what she was going to do about it.

Chapter Twenty-Two

Jim was left to stare morosely into his coffee cup. His flatmates had walked in to find him practically shouting at the girl. He should have known better, he thought. Yelling at her wasn't going to help the situation.

The thing was, she had scared him badly last night. It wasn't just that he felt responsible for her. He sympathised with her. It was fairly clear what that woman had said was something Amanda had been already thinking anyway, judging from what he'd heard in his boss' office.

The worst part for him was the thought that something much worse could have happened than her getting drunk and sleeping with some random guy. Jim knew from experience just how bad it could get, from someone being killed in a drunken fight with another person, to young girls being raped.

"Mate, you were kind of harsh with her, don't you think?"

He looked up at Craig. "What?"

"You were just about screaming at her," his flatmate told him. Susan nodded her agreement.

"Was that the girl you told us about?" she asked.

He cupped the back of his neck, tilting his head back with a tired sigh.

"Yeah."

"So what happened to get you so angry?" Craig asked.

He told them as much as he could without giving specifics of the case.

"What upsets you more? The fact that you saw her with this other guy or that she could have got herself into a very dangerous situation?" Susan asked.

"What?" he asked, staring at her.

"Well, it seems to me that you didn't like her kissing this other man. I wonder if perhaps you like her more than you're willing to admit."

"No, that's not it," he told them. Or was it? he thought. He hadn't exactly pushed her away when she'd tried to lay one on him.

"Look, we get it," Craig said. "Your friend hasn't handled things well, but you're not exactly blameless. It's called kicking someone when they're down. True, she could have come off a lot worse than just a bad hangover, but screaming at her wouldn't have helped either."

"I know," he said with a long sigh. "I know." He'd known from the way she reacted, as if she'd been slapped, that he had gone too far. "The question is, what can I do about it?"

Craig sighed. "If I knew that, I'd be richer than Midas."

Jim shot his flatmate a doleful look. "Oh gee, that's helpful."

He glanced at the clock, seeing from the time he was going to be late for work if he didn't get moving. He was sure his boss would understand, however, since he had spent half the night looking for Amanda.

He showered and shaved before dressing for work in black wool trousers and a clean sky-blue shirt. His last girlfriend had always admired him in the shirt, saying it brought out the blue in his eyes. He still had fond thoughts of his ex-girlfriend although they had only dated a few months. They'd ended things on fairly good terms. He'd often wondered why she never called him unless she wanted something but his stepmother had told him she was probably just shy. It made sense, he thought, looking back at the way she reacted to certain things.

Amanda reminded him a little of his ex. They were both smart and very attractive. Linda had had a great sense of humour and so did Amanda in her own way. His parents had liked Linda, expressing the hope that he had found someone he could settle down with. As much as he had liked spending time with her, Jim hadn't been able to see a future with her.

The segue reminded him he needed to call his parents. Lesleigh usually called him once a week just to see how he was doing. He knew he should try to call them more often than he did, but there were times when he was just too busy.

There was a note on his desk when he finally got into work, an hour and a half after he was supposed to have started. Mark Gerraghty wanted to see him.

He sighed. The last thing he wanted to do was sit in a meeting with his boss. While he wasn't expected to just hang around the station, especially with his caseload, he wanted to focus on finding Lori Mattison's killer. Or killers, he thought. Despite Billy's analysis being inconclusive, Jim thought there was no way she'd been killed by one person acting alone.

He got up from his desk, heading back out through the bullpen to the waiting area. Kerry looked up from the fishbowl, one eyebrow cocked.

"Boss wants to see me," he said.

"He's on a call right now," Kerry told him. "You'll have to wait." She seemed a little cool and he wondered why. He didn't have to wait long for an answer.

"Amanda's my friend," she said.

"Your point being?" he asked, deciding to return the cool attitude.

"Meaning she tells me everything, and I do mean everything."

"So she told you about the case?"

"Well, no, but she did call me this morning. In tears. Amanda's a tough kid and it takes a lot to make her cry."

He felt an odd sensation in his stomach, as if he'd suddenly fallen down a long drop. Guilt, he thought. He really needed to call her and apologise for yelling at her.

Still, part of him wouldn't let go the fact that she had brought on the problem herself.

"Well, maybe if you had seen the state she was in last night, you wouldn't be so quick to judge," he replied defensively.

Kerry looked taken aback. She might be only twenty-five but Kerry Marshall had been working at the station for five years. She had clearly earned the respect of her colleagues. It meant they didn't talk back to her the way he had just done.

She had no opportunity to reply as the door to the area commander's office opened and Mark came out. He nodded at Jim.

"Detective Andersen. Come in." He glanced at Kerry. "Could you call Pete and remind him, please?"

Jim followed his boss into the office and sat down in one of the chairs opposite the huge oak desk. The sun was shining in the windows, causing him to squint at the brightness. Mark made no move to close the blinds, which made Jim wonder if he was in for an interrogation.

His boss sat down but didn't speak. Instead he looked at the screen of his laptop, his hand resting on the wireless mouse. The occasional click was the only sound inside the room, which was growing stuffier by the minute. Jim fought the urge to pull at his shirt collar.

It was probably only a couple of minutes but it felt like hours when Pete finally walked in. The inspector gestured toward the other seat in the room. His immediate superior looked a little worried, which only served to heighten Jim's nervousness.

Mark finally looked up and smiled at them.

"Relax boys, this is not the Spanish Inquisition."

"That remains to be seen," Pete muttered.

Their boss chuckled. "Pete, you know me better than that. We've been working together for how long?"

"A long time."

The other man was about five or six years older than the detective sergeant. He had transferred to the West Side station about five years earlier, having served in other cities around the country before being promoted to area commander.

"In all seriousness, though, I'm concerned. How did your daughter happen to get mixed up in all this business at Fraley High?"

"I'm afraid that was an administrative decision at the school," Pete explained. "I've known Matt Donaldson for a number of years. He expressed to me his concerns about the school and the various goings-on there but he wasn't willing to risk his job by involving police."

"Yet he knows there has been criminal activity there."

"Knowing it and actually providing physical evidence is another thing. There are a couple of parents on the school board who think they know the law better than we do and Matt feared if he called us they would force him to resign so they could bring in someone else who was willing to overlook the problems."

"I understand the previous principal was fired for similar reasons," Mark replied. "Yes, I see your point. Still, Amanda is hardly experienced."

"That was sort of the point too. Her job was to get close to the students and see what she could find out. It was supposed to be a simple observation."

The inspector looked at Jim.

"So, what's your take on the situation?"

"Sir, I have to admit I had my doubts Amanda could pull this off. As you said, she's not very experienced in this type of work. I was concerned when she told me she had concocted a story to cover why she was there, but I went along with it because Pete asked me to help out. She's a good kid but way too green and somebody had to keep an eye on things."

"True, but now we have a big problem with this girl being murdered. What have you discovered so far?"

"Not much. I have my suspicions as to who was behind it but as far as motive goes ..."

"Have you questioned the suspects?"

"We pulled them in for questioning the day the victim was found but we weren't aware at that time it was an actual homicide. I sent Dave to bring them in yesterday but they weren't home. They haven't been to school either."

Pete spoke up. "I've already sought a warrant for their arrests," he said.

Mark nodded. "Good. The sooner we get this dreadful matter cleared up the better. The local paper is already having a field day. Did you see the story on their webpage this morning?"

Jim shook his head. He hadn't bothered to check the local media.

"I know the reporter at the local paper," Pete interjected. "She's not the problem. She's been there a long time and we trust her. It's her editor. The man has his head up his ass, and that's the polite term for it."

"The national paper's worse," Mark said with a groan. "The way their story reads, I'm just a lazy cop with his head in the sand. Although, to be honest, I didn't like being kept in the dark about this."

Pete ducked his head, looking shamefaced. "Well, boss, it's not like we expected this turn of events. I did advise you as soon as things started to turn bad."

The commander nodded and sat back, looking more relaxed. They talked for a little while longer, discussing where to go next. Jim emerged from the meeting feeling assured that his boss wasn't too displeased with them.

When he got back to the bullpen he found a new message on his desk telling him to phone his parents. He sighed and picked up the phone.

"Hello darling," Lesleigh said when she picked up. "What is this about a murder and why is the local paper calling for heads to roll?"

Jim swallowed hard. This must be what Mark had been talking about.

"Uh, Mum, it's not really like that."

"Well, according to this editor, there have been two deaths at this school and police have been sitting on their asses, quote, unquote, doing nothing."

"What?" he said.

He logged on to his computer and immediately accessed the editorial. His eyes darted back and forth rapidly as he read the text. The editorial was scathing, claiming police knew the school was practically a hive of criminal activity but were doing nothing about it.

Luckily the editor hadn't learnt about Amanda's firm's involvement in the case. The criticism was bad enough without someone suggesting that Amanda was doing their job for them.

"This thing is getting worse all the time," he muttered.

Chapter Twenty-Three

Amanda hesitantly knocked on the door. Normally she would just walk straight in, but for some reason she felt a little uneasy.

Her father looked surprised to see her when he opened the door.

"What'd you knock for?" he asked.

He was still wearing his work clothes. Normally when he finished his shift he liked to go home and relax with a beer. At least on normal weeknights. Clearly he hadn't been home that long. He was wearing reading glasses, something he had once avoided out of either vanity or just a refusal to admit he was getting old.

"Dad, I ..."

He peered at her over the tops of his glasses, his brow furrowing in concern.

"Come in, honey. What's wrong?"

She followed him in, spotting the papers on the table as she stepped through the small entrance way to the open-plan living area. Bills, she thought.

"Want something to drink?"

She shook her head. After what had happened the other night, the last thing she wanted to touch was alcohol of any kind.

"What's going on, sweetheart?"

She thrust her hands in her jacket pockets and bit her lip while trying to avoid his concerned gaze.

"Dad, I ... I did something really stupid."

He nodded. "Jim beat you to it. He told me what happened the other night."

She stared at him, wondering why he was so calm about it. He picked up his bottle of beer from the table and shrugged.

"Jim called me after you took off and asked if I knew any of your hangouts. After what happened, I was afraid you might get into trouble." He offered her a wry smile. "I was right, wasn't I?"

She looked at him, expecting a scolding. Anything but calm reason.

"You're not yelling."

He cocked an eyebrow.

"Do you expect me to? Amanda, you're nineteen, and while I do sometimes still see you as my little girl, you are an adult and responsible for your own choices.

"Although," he added, "I'm a little surprised it took you until tonight to come and see me. Am I that much of an ogre?"

She was forced to smile at her father's weak attempt at humour.

"No, Daddy," she said, running her finger along the table. "I was just ... ashamed. I was ... what I did, it was really stupid. Jim yelled at me."

He nodded. "Yes, I know about that too. He's sorry he yelled at you, by the way. He admitted he might have over-reacted."

She bit her lip. Part of her had been hurt that Jim had said all those things to her while another part of her wondered if she had deserved it. She knew better than to let a strange man buy drinks for her. Even if the guy had been a good listener.

She recalled telling DJ all about the case and her desire to be a cop once the whiskey had loosened her up. He had listened, only talking when it seemed she had run out of things to say, prompting her to say more. Come to think of it, she had done most of the talking all night, getting less lucid the drunker she became.

She really should have known better than to blurt out all her secrets to a guy she'd only just met. He could have been anyone. She really was naïve as Jim had once accused.

The last thing she remembered was DJ asking her if she wanted to go somewhere else.

"I was so stupid, Dad."

He looked her over with a sympathetic expression.

"Do you want me to admonish you? Send you to your room, so to speak? Amanda, you made a mistake. At least you didn't get into anything. Or did you?"

Her memory might be hazy but she was fairly sure she hadn't done anything other than what Jim had witnessed. Her father had taught her what to do when she'd turned eighteen and been old enough to go out to nightclubs. She knew not to accept drinks from strangers and to never drink anything unless she got it herself.

She'd broken every one of those rules in the past few days, since before Lori ... The realisation hit her.

"Oh god, I'm an idiot!" she said to herself.

Her father was shooting her an odd look, clearly wondering what she was thinking.

"I think I'd know if anything like that happened," she told him, choosing not to explain. "I mean, I don't sleep with random guys!" She sighed. "Okay, the other night was a big mistake and I know that, but I think I'd know if I lost my virginity!"

He lowered his bottle and stared at her.

"You mean you've never ..."

She stared back at him. "What?"

"Not once?"

"Oh my god, I can't believe my own father thinks I'm a slut!"

He spluttered, coughing for a few seconds before replying.

"Don't put words in my mouth! You have to admit you had a few boyfriends ..."

She felt her cheeks growing hot and knew she was blushing beet red with embarrassment. What a conversation to be having with her own father!

"Friends, Dad! I had a total of one actual boyfriend, whom I dumped by the way, when he tried to get too handsy. I wasn't ready to sleep with him and he didn't like it, so I said sayonara. Did you really think I was sleeping around in high school?"

"Well, honey, you do tend to come across as rather, uh, bold!"

She stared at him, completely flummoxed.

"So, over-confidence is akin to promiscuity? Gee, feeling the love in this room!"

"You're right. I'm sorry. I was making a bad assumption." He wrapped an arm around her and kissed her on the top of her head.

"Forgive your old man. He still sees you as the little girl he bounced on his knee and not a young woman mature enough to know her own mind. I don't think I was ever ready for the sex talk." He scratched at his lip. "So, totally nosy, but ... why?"

"Why what?"

"Why have you never ...?"

The heat in her cheeks was back but she took a deep breath and let it out slowly.

"I don't know. I just never found the right guy, I guess."

"Well, that's rather refreshing. You know, the statistics ..."

"I don't need to hear the statistics, Daddy! Besides, it's my body, and I figure if I ... when I sleep with someone it'll be because I really care about him. Not because of peer pressure."

"That's very mature of you honey."

"It's just ... I worry sometimes."

"About what?"

"Well, what if I never meet him? You know, the guy who ... well, rocks my world?"

He raised an eyebrow, his lips twitching, clearly amused by the phrasing.

"Trust me, honey, you don't always know right away. Sometimes it just takes a while for you to open your eyes to the possibilities."

She studied him for a moment.

"Did you know? With Mum?"

He canted his head. "Right away? No. Your mum and I were friends first. It took a while for us to realise."

She nodded and thought about her mother and the way she had left. Amanda remembered her parents fighting and the sound of her father's pleas as her mother packed her bags and walked out.

"Did you ever go looking for Mum?" she asked.

He nodded. "I had colleagues looking up and down the country for her. We asked around for about eight months but your mother didn't want to be found."

"Why did she leave anyway?" She knew what had been behind her mother's leaving, but it still didn't tell her why.

"She was sick, honey. I suppose she just wanted to save us the grief of trying to take care of her when she couldn't even take care of herself." He looked at her. "Your mum would be so proud of you."

She shrugged. She knew he was trying to protect her from what had happened, but didn't have the heart to tell him the truth. Better to preserve the illusion that she was ignorant of her mother's problems.

She had no idea if her mother even knew what she was doing. There were the occasional birthday cards but while they had been postmarked from various towns, there had never been a return address.

"I guess."

She hugged her father. "Thanks for the talk, Daddy."

He smiled. "Any time honey."

She moved to the door then looked at him.

"Um, do you think I should, uh, talk to Jim?" She chewed on her lower lip. "I mean, is he still mad at me?"

"I don't think he was ever really mad at you, sweetheart. Just worried. I do think you two need to clear the air though."

She nodded. "Yeah. You're right. 'Night Dad."

Chapter Twenty-Four

Jim was surprised to see Amanda on his doorstep. After the way he had behaved toward her the other morning, he had half-expected her to avoid him.

"Hi," she said, looking more than a little uncertain. She thrust her hands in the pockets of her denim jacket. Jim heard the faint jingle of keys as they shifted. He was a little lost for words so he just stared at her.

"Um, can I come in?" she asked.

He held the door open. "Uh, sure."

She stepped over the threshold and followed him down the little hallway to the kitchen. He thought about cracking a joke but she looked ill at ease. As if she wasn't comfortable in her own skin.

He moved into the kitchen and leaned on the counter as she stood in the middle of the dining area, kicking the table leg and looking down at the floor.

"So, what's up?" he asked. She remained quiet, not saying anything. They both stood as if waiting for something. She fidgeted nervously.

"Amanda?" he asked.

"I just came from my dad's," she said, finally looking at him. "I … I mean, we … uh …"

He frowned at her, not sure what seeing her dad had to do with anything.

"God, this is stupid," she muttered. "I'm sorry. I shouldn't have … I mean, my dad said you're not, but you probably are mad at me and you have every right to be. I mean, what I did the other night was totally stupid and I know better and if it wasn't for you, God knows what I would have got into." She stopped babbling. "I should go."

He moved quickly to stop her as she turned on her heel and headed for the front door. He grasped her by the shoulders, halting her.

"Now wait a minute. You can't come in here and ramble on, mumble some half-assed apology and expect that to make up for everything that happened the other night."

She seemed to be on the verge of tears, refusing to look at him.

"You're right," she agreed quietly.

"Amanda, that's not what I meant. Yes, what happened was bad, but I over-reacted. I shouldn't have yelled at you yesterday."

She pulled away and walked over to the huge glass pane in the sliding door. The lights in the room contrasted with the darkness outside, showing her reflection on the glass. She appeared to flinch as she saw her pale face and huge eyes.

"You okay?" he asked quietly.

She turned away from the door and looked up at him, shrugging her shoulders.

"Honestly? Not really. I've been doing a lot of thinking, the last couple days. I really screwed up, Jim. I went into this thinking it would be a piece of cake, but the truth is, I have no idea what the hell I'm doing." She sniffled.

"I don't know what to do. I can't drop it and let Donaldson or Mr Moody down. But I'm in over my head."

Jim remembered what Amanda's friend had told him the day before. Amanda was tough and rarely cried. At least, not in front of anyone. Not even her father. She was crying now, however. Silent tears were running down her cheeks.

Part of him wondered if she was trying to con him into helping her. She could be a devious little minx when she wanted to be, and he wouldn't have been surprised if she was turning on the waterworks just to get his sympathy.

Stuff it, he thought, wrapping his arms around her in a comforting hug. So what if she was conning him?

She relaxed in his arms, pressing her face against his chest. Her voice was muffled as she spoke.

"This doesn't make us friends though," she said.

"I know," he replied, rubbing her back. "We'll just keep this a secret between us."

He heard her snort and it seemed like a giggle escaped. Okay, so maybe she wasn't a complete pain in the ass, he thought.

"Want a drink?" he asked, then regretted the suggestion immediately.

She lifted her head and looked at him for a long moment, then nodded.

"As long as it's non-alcoholic," she replied. She gestured an emphatic 'no' with her hands. "No way am I getting myself into that kind of trouble again."

"Coffee?" he asked, heading for the kitchen to switch on the coffee pot.

"Yeah. Sounds good."

Jim quickly made the coffee and gestured for her to precede him into the living room where they sat in recliners.

"So ..." he said, sipping his coffee. "What are you going to do?"

"I can't just drop it," she repeated. "Lori died because of me."

He frowned at her. "How do you figure that?"

"I don't know. It's just a feeling."

Amanda might be young, but if there was one thing he did know, it was that she had good instincts. He tried to get her to follow her train of thought.

"Is there anything you might have noticed the other night which might make you feel that way? What about Kyle?"

"I'm not sure."

"Okay, well, let's go over it again. Tell me everything you can remember from the night Lori died. You said you went to a bar. Which one?"

She told him. Jim nodded. There had been a few

incidents at that particular nightspot, not only with underage drinking but a couple of staff were suspected drug dealers.

"What happened the other night?" he prompted Amanda. "The night Lori died, I mean."

She bit her lip, then sipped her coffee, taking the time to think about her answer.

"Well, I went to the bar thinking I could watch them. Maybe catch Kyle and Jake in the act, so to speak. Lori came in and saw me and acted like she wanted me to leave."

"Any idea why she might have done that?"

"I don't know. She seemed anxious. She kept looking toward the door."

"Okay, then what?"

"Well, then Kyle and Jake showed up and Jake pulled her away while Kyle offered to buy me a beer."

He frowned. He remembered Amanda saying something about this before, but it seemed anomalous. The impression he had was that Amanda disliked Kyle intensely and the feeling was mutual.

"Why would Kyle offer to buy you a beer if he didn't like you? Come to that, why would you let him?"

"I don't know. I just figured I'd see what he was up to."

He shook his head. She should have known better than to let a guy like Kyle buy her a beer. Her eyes widened as she clearly realised what he was thinking.

"I wasn't going to drink it!" she replied. "I don't even like beer! Besides, Lori spilled it so it's kind of irrelevant."

He frowned, going over the events in his head and trying to figure out how they would have led to Lori's death. Something about this just wasn't making sense. There was something missing.

"Amanda, I shouldn't be telling you this, but Lori had GHB in her system."

She stared at him. "What?"

"GHB. It's a compound often used in ..."

"I know what it's used for," she said. "My dad gave me a pamphlet to read up on date rape drugs when I turned eighteen."

She lapsed into silence and leaned back in the chair while sipping her coffee. Suddenly she sat up gasping, almost spilling the rest of her drink.

"What?"

"I think I know why Lori spilled the beer!"

Chapter Twenty-Five

The talk with Jim had helped in a lot of ways. Going over exactly what had happened the night Lori died had helped her get some perspective and see things from another angle.

She went home and immediately went to the bathroom, hoping to find the top she'd thrown into the bin the other night. When she found it empty, she called out Penny's name. When her flatmate didn't reply, Amanda went to her room and knocked on the door. "Penny?" she called.

"What?"

Amanda opened the door. Her flatmate was sitting up in bed watching television. She stared at her.

"Did you empty the bin in the bathroom?"

The older woman scowled as if to imply Amanda was interrupting something important.

"Well, yeah. You're always nagging me about taking the rubbish out. So I did. Why?"

"Nothing. Never mind."

Damn, she thought, sighing. Well, it was a long shot. She had hoped that if she still had the top it could be analysed for any residue, but there was only a small chance that it would have shown up in the fibres.

She had told Jim about the bar and her suspicions about its practices. She was fairly sure one of the staff was dealing, after what she had witnessed two weeks earlier. Jim had advised her there wasn't much to go on but she still felt it was worth checking out.

She still had one other option, she decided as she grabbed her car keys. Jim had told her about the joyriding pair and she was thankful they had been caught. Her car might not be modern or cool, being fifteen years old, but she had earned the money to pay for it by working at MacDonald's for three years.

Friday nights tended to be the worst time to try to find a park in the inner city, especially around the local nightspots. Amanda found herself driving around the streets, circling the block a few times before someone pulled out of a parking spot. She parked her car and locked the steering wheel with a double hook locking device before getting out and activating the alarm.

The bar where she had met Lori and the others the week before was close to the waterfront. It was just as crowded as it had been the weekend before, with the usual group of teens standing outside smoking. The bouncer on the door looked bored. He barely glanced at her as she passed him to enter the bar.

She looked around, squinting her eyes in the dim lighting. At least a dozen people were lined up against the bar but none of them appeared to be familiar. There were three bar staff serving. Again none of them were the one she wanted to talk to.

She continued looking around, then spotted a small group at a table in the far corner. Two boys and a girl. They were all sitting around the table, talking quietly with a pitcher of beer in front of them.

The group hung out with Kyle and Jake at the school. Amanda doubted they knew much about the boys' activities, but they weren't exactly innocent either.

Amanda made her way through the throng of people to the table. The girl looked up with an expression of surprise, then scowled at her.

"What are you doing here?" she asked crossly.

"Looking for Kyle and Jake," Amanda replied. "Are they here?"

"What are you, stupid?" a boy whose name she couldn't remember growled. "Don't you know the cops are after them?"

"Yeah," the girl replied. "The cops have been all over school. Looking for drugs."

"As if we'd be stupid enough to ..." the second youth began. "Where've you been? Cops been after you too?"

She didn't reply, spotting one of the bar staff crossing the floor after picking up empty glasses from various tables.

"I gotta go," she said, turning away from them.

"Whatever!" The tone suggested they didn't care either way.

She followed the man as he took the tray to the kitchen, then headed toward the back door. Figuring he was headed toward the alley, Amanda turned around and left the bar by the front door, making her way around the back.

Sure enough, he was standing by the door, smoking a cigarette and talking to one of the other staff members. He spotted her and nodded his head in her direction. The pair stared at her as she approached them.

"What do you want?"

"I'm looking for Kyle," she said.

"Kyle who?" the man asked.

"Oh, don't play dumb," she said. "I've seen you out here with them before."

"Don't know what you're talking about," he replied, throwing his half-smoked cigarette toward her. Amanda quickly side-stepped and grabbed his arm before he could go back inside.

"We need to talk," she told him.

He looked down at her hand on his arm and smirked.

"Yeah? What about?" he asked before leading her away from the door and the others watching.

She studied him. He was only about eighteen by her reckoning. His face was covered in acne which only served to make him look younger. Even without the acne he wasn't someone she would be interested in.

That didn't stop him from assuming that was what she wanted. He crowded her, pushing her against the brick wall, one hand crawling up her side to cup her breast.

Amanda wanted to vomit from his fetid breath. Instead, she grabbed his wrist and twisted his arm away from his body so he was forced to turn with it or risk injury. She used her other hand to shove him back. He was tall but skinny and clearly not used to girls fighting back.

"Listen jerkoff, I'm not playing games here. I know you're involved in some little scam with Kyle and some of his buddies. So I'm gonna give you one chance."

He struggled in her grip. "Damn, you're strong for a girl."

"And I'm gonna rip your nuts off if you don't tell me what I want to know."

His eyes widened. "It's not ... I mean, I just slip the stuff in the drinks. That's it."

"What stuff?" she asked, lifting her knee and pressing it against his stomach. He closed his eyes, screwing up his face.

"Aghhh, don't do that. Come on, lady!"

"What stuff?" she asked, pressing just a little bit harder. He grunted.

"You know. The stuff. It gets the girls all, you know, relaxed."

Relaxed my ass, she thought. They were drugging them.

"Where are they getting it from?"

"I don't know," he said. She pushed down, making him gasp in alarm. "I don't know, I swear," he repeated, squeezing his eyes shut.

She heard the sound of voices, then looked up to see Stu Dawson watching her with a smirk.

"I'll take it from here," he said. She noticed he had his cuffs out. "You're under arrest," he told the youth, moving toward them.

Amanda let the youth go and stood back. He opened his eyes and stared in shock at the uniformed officers. He offered no resistance as he was cuffed.

"You know, mate, you're lucky she <u>didn't</u> rip your balls off."

Amanda spotted Jim talking to the bouncer as she followed the officers. He nodded at her and waved her away.

Not sure what to do next, she decided to start walking back to her car. As she reached the end of the walkway past the clubs, she saw two taxis waiting at a nearby taxi stand.

"Of course!" she said to herself.

She ran up to the first driver, noting the taxi was from the same company the driver from the night Lori had been killed had contracted for.

"Hi, I need your help. I need to track down one of your drivers."

The man looked at her with an odd expression. Amanda had heard of a few taxi drivers being attacked and she assumed the driver was worried about the same thing happening.

"I lost my cell phone in a taxi," she lied. "I don't remember the driver's name, just what he looked like. He was wearing a turban." She thought for a few seconds. "Oh, and he said he's saving up to buy his own restaurant."

The man brightened. "That's Gundar," he replied. "But I don't know where he is."

"Can you get on your radio and find out? I really need that cell phone."

He nodded and picked up the transmitter, speaking into it. The answer came back after about a minute.

"He's on his break, but he will be back on duty in about fifteen minutes. He will come straight here."

Amanda smiled at the man. "Thank you. Thank you so much."

She found somewhere to sit and watch the taxi stand while she waited for Gundar. A few other taxis picked up passengers but none of the drivers had turbans.

About twenty minutes later, a driver wearing a turban pulled up outside. A woman standing at the taxi stand reached for the door, but the driver shook his head. Amanda approached the door.

"Thanks, but this is my taxi," she replied.

"I was here first!" the woman said crossly.

"Well I've been waiting twenty minutes. There are plenty of other taxis." She stared the woman down, then got in the front seat. Gundar looked at her.

"You are not the girl who lost the cell phone," he said in his accented English. "You are the girl with the shirt."

"Yes, I'm sorry for the little deception. I needed to talk to you. Will you please drive up the street a little? My car is parked a few streets away."

He frowned at her, clearly wondering why she needed a taxi if her car was not that far away. Amanda handed him twenty dollars for his trouble.

"Please," she said. "This is important."

"All right."

She waited until he had pulled up beside her car before turning to him.

"You told me the other night you picked up a young girl about four in the morning."

"Yes."

"What did this girl look like? Can you remember?"

He nodded. "Oh yes, I remember. She was young, younger than you, I think. Very small. She was very upset and did not look well."

"Yes, you said that. What about her appearance? Did anything stand out about her?"

"No, well, yes, she had hair the colour of a sunset. I only know this because I had never seen a girl with such colour hair before."

"Emma," Amanda said to herself. Gundar looked at her with a puzzled expression.

"Excuse me?" he asked.

"I think I do know this girl," she said. "Where is the cell phone you found?"

He reached over to the glove box and pulled out the phone. It was a cheap Alcatel android phone. The screen was badly cracked. Amanda wasn't sure if it would still work.

"Can I ask why you need this?"

"If I'm right about who owns this phone, she's the victim in a very bad scheme. Gundar, I'm going to need to give your details to the police. They may need you as a witness."

He looked alarmed. "The police? I don't understand."

"I'm sorry," she said. "I work for a private investigator. I've been looking into a case and this girl is just one of many I suspect have been caught up in it. You're not in trouble, I assure you."

"All right," he replied. "What will you do with that?"

"I'm going to give it to a friend of mine in the police," she told him as she reached for the door. "Thanks again for your help."

She got out of the car, waving him off, before unlocking her own car. She debated what to do. She wondered if Jim had decided to check out her story or whether something else had brought him to the bar. It didn't matter, she thought.

She decided to drive to her father's place despite the late hour, figuring he would know what to do with the phone.

It was obvious he had been asleep as he looked at her blearily His bathrobe was half-open, showing a bare chest. Amanda pretended not to notice. The last thing she wanted to imagine was her middle-aged father sleeping naked. Ugh, she thought, suppressing a shudder. Her dad might be a good-looking man and not that old but that was just ... ick!

"Daddy, I'm sorry. I know it's really late, or early, but ..."

"What's going on?" he asked.

She showed him the cell phone. He frowned at her.

"Honey ..."

"I doubt you're going to get much in the way of prints," she told him. "If you get any data off it though, it might help the case."

He still looked confused. "How did you get hold of this?"

She told him about being picked up by the taxi driver the night Lori was killed and the story the man had told her. Then she related how she had tracked down the man and asked for the phone.

"You're sure this belongs to ..."

"I'm ninety-nine percent sure," she told him. He shot her a look. "Okay, ninety percent." Another look. "Fine," she said, sighing. "Eighty."

"Honey, things get lost in taxis all the time."

"Yeah, but how many get cracked like that while sitting in the back of a taxi? I mean, why would someone take a broken phone with them?"

"You're assuming ..."

"Call it a hunch, Dad. Look, you're always saying I should use my instincts more and my instincts are telling me that that phone belonged to Emma. Oh, I got the driver's card. He might be a witness."

She gave him the phone and the card, kissing him on the cheek. "Thanks Dad."

He spluttered. "You're welcome?"

Chapter Twenty-Six

Jim was in the office early despite the late night. He hadn't been rostered on but since he had a homicide to solve, he ignored the roster.

He hadn't planned on going out the night before, but after the things Amanda had told him about the bar, he had decided it was worth checking it out. Amanda had presumably not seen him come in as she had dashed past him without acknowledging his presence.

He figured the three youths she had been talking to had decided things were getting a little too hot for them when the uniformed officers showed up. Jim drew Dawson aside after he'd arrested the bartender.

"Who called you?" he asked.

Dawson shook his head. "We were in the area anyway. There are always fights outside this place so we check it on a regular basis."

Jim wanted to take him to task for ignoring the underage drinking but they had bigger things to worry about. Judging from what Amanda had managed to get out of the youth they'd arrested, there was a lot more going on than underage drinking. Something far more sinister.

"'Morning," a deep voice said tiredly. Jim looked up and frowned at his boss, who flopped in the chair beside the desk.

"Uh, morning," he said. "I thought this was your weekend off?"

"Tell that to my daughter who decided to pay me a midnight visit." He groaned. "I swear sometimes I could strangle her."

He placed a plastic bag containing an android phone on the desk. Jim picked up the bag, frowning as he noticed the badly cracked screen.

"Don't waste your time getting fingerprints off it," Pete said. "There are probably so many you won't get anything decent."

"Where did this ..."

"Amanda thinks it belonged to the girlfriend of that young man, Mitchell. She said a taxi driver found it after he took a girl matching Emma's description home."

Jim frowned at him. "I'm still not following."

"Me either. She's following a hunch."

Jim groaned, rubbing his face with one hand. "She lives to drive me crazy," he said.

"How do you think I feel?" Pete said wryly. "I raised her! What does that say about me?"

"That you have the patience of a saint," he returned, grinning at the detective sergeant. "I'll give this to our tech guys and see what they can get off it. If anything."

"Good. Now tell me what's been going on."

"Well, I hate to say it, but we've got your daughter to thank for an arrest we made last night. Seems there was this kid at the Rover who was in on the scam with our two suspects. She confronted him."

"You interviewed him yet?"

Jim shook his head. "Not yet. I've got him cooling his heels in the cells."

"We still need to find those two boys."

"Yeah, I know." He told his boss about Amanda's visit the night before and his decision to check out the bar.

"Any idea who these kids are?"

"No, we don't have any records on them, but it's not hard to guess they go to Fraley. I left a message on Matt Donaldson's phone to bring in some student files."

"Well, good. Let's keep the momentum going, Jim. The sooner we sort this mess out the happier I will be."

Jim nodded, getting the impression that his boss was still worried about his daughter. Given the way she seemed to be running about trying to solve the case, he had every right to be concerned.

Gathering his notes together, Jim called down to the cells to have the suspect brought up to an interview room. He then got up from his desk and left the bullpen.

The young man was sitting at the table, looking a little nervous. A uniformed constable stood stiffly beside him. Jim dropped the file on the table with a slap and nodded to the constable, who nodded in reply and left the room, closing the door softly behind him.

"So, Eddie, I hear you like to drug girls."

"I'm not saying anything," the youth said sullenly. "I want a lawyer."

"Your duty solicitor will be along shortly," Jim said. "Right now, I just want to have a little chat with you. I hope you realise the seriousness of the charges facing you. Grievous bodily harm, accessory to murder ..."

Eddie started. "What? I didn't murder anyone! Where does it say that?" He reached for the folder on the table but Jim quickly moved it away.

"How do you know Kyle Thomas?"

The boy shrugged. "We sort of hung out. At school."

"Fraley High?"

"He got left back a year."

"I see."

"Look, whatever that says I did, you're wrong."

"So you're denying the fact that you confessed to putting dangerous narcotics in the drinks of young women?"

"Uh ... Look, that girl, she's trouble, okay?"

"Define the word, 'trouble'."

"I don't know. I mean, Kyle told me to ... you know, slip a little something. He just wanted her out of the way."

"A little something?" Jim repeated. "Why did Kyle want her out of the way?"

The youth shrugged. "Kyle didn't tell me. He just told me to slip a pill into a beer."

Well, that partly explained what had happened that night, Jim thought. It still didn't give him any clue as to Lori's motivation for spilling the beer, but he realised Amanda had guessed the beer had been drugged. She had had a very lucky escape that night.

He glared at the bartender.

"So what? Kyle gives the orders and you just do as you're told? What did you get out of this?"

"Well, sometimes I'd get, you know, a little taste. Mostly they'd give me money."

"Where did they get the stuff from?"

"I don't know. Like I told that girl last night I really don't know. They never told me."

He paused and looked at Jim. "What's going to happen to me?"

Jim said nothing, half-afraid he would strangle the kid for what he'd been participating in. He glared at him with narrowed eyes.

You knew they were drugging and raping young girls and you sat back and did nothing, he accused the youth silently. You deserve to rot in hell you little shit!

He looked up at a knock on the door. A short, dumpy woman with straight brown hair left in a loose style entered the room. She was dressed in a wool suit and carried a briefcase. This must be the duty solicitor, he thought.

"I'm advising you not to say anything further, Eddie." She looked sternly at Jim and handed him a business card, indicating her role in these proceedings. "You wouldn't be questioning my client and ignoring due process, would you?"

"Of course not," he told her before returning his gaze to the eighteen-year-old bartender.

"How long have you been working at Rover, Eddie?"

The youth shrugged. "Couple months. I know the owner through a friend of a friend. It's just a part-time gig while I'm studying."

Jim knew with the charges facing this young man the likelihood of him actually completing his studies - at least in the next few years - was going to be between slim and none. He really didn't seem to care what he'd become involved in, or for the victims. Although they still had to find those victims.

"Where is Kyle, Eddie?"

"I don't know man. He took off last week and I haven't heard from him. We were s'posed to meet up Sunday but he never showed."

Gee, wonder why, Jim thought, considering that was the morning Lori had been found. He wasn't surprised Kyle had just vanished. It was more than likely he was on the run.

"Are you done?" the solicitor asked.

Jim glared at her, unfazed by the narrowed brown eyes glaring back at him. From what he had heard, Tess McCloskey was considered something of a dragon, even in her own office. While it was his first time dealing with her, he wasn't about to let himself be intimidated by a woman at least a head shorter than him.

"For now," he said coolly. "I will leave you with this though, Eddie. You're in a hell of a lot of trouble. If you tell us what you know, it might help your case." He got up and went to the door, opening it before turning to look at the youth. "Think about it."

Okay, so he was bluffing about what they actually knew. Most of it they were only assuming, but given the combination of drugs that had killed Lori Mattison and the incident Amanda had described, it wasn't that difficult to make the connection.

When he got back to his desk, he saw he had missed a call on his phone. It was an internal extension, one he recognised from the I.T. department, such as it was. Like every other police station in the country, their operating budgets had taken a huge hit. While the national powers-that-be thought more emphasis should be placed on police being more visible in the public and more mobility, they tended to forget that the only way to do so was by giving them access to the right technology.

Jim dialled the extension but got no reply. Sighing, he got up again and headed downstairs to the offices of Technical Services, otherwise known as the Geek Squad.

Only one person was in the office, working on a laptop. The girl was pretty, with short dark hair. She wore something that reminded Jim a little of a Viewmaster toy he had had when he was a child. Except that it was secured with a headband so the person could use both hands while working.

She looked up. Jim could see her eyes looked huge beneath the lenses.

"Uh, hi?" he said uncertainly, disconcerted by the way her eyes seemed five times bigger than normal.

She blinked rapidly, then pulled the magnifying goggles off and shook her head.

"Sorry. Sometimes I get so caught up in what I'm doing that I forget I'm wearing them. What's up?"

"Uh, I think you called me," he said.

"Oh! Yeah! I had a look at that cell phone. It's pretty much shot, but I did manage to download some data off it."

She swung around in her chair and tapped on the plasma screen behind her, swiping across to bring up an image. Jim leaned forward to get a closer look. Some of the data had been corrupted, but he could see pieces of a few photos.

"Are you able to re-render those photos?"

She cocked an eyebrow at him. "I'm a tech geek, not a miracle worker." He fought the urge to laugh. She obviously knew her section was called the Geek Squad, plus he gave her points for the Star Trek reference. She was cute. Geeks had certainly changed since he was in high school.

"Could you at least try?" he asked imploringly. "I mean, there must be something you can do."

She shook her head. "Sorry. No. Not in such a short timeframe anyway. It would take me a month of Sundays. Afraid it's not as easy as pushing a button."

He sighed. "Well, is there anything useable?"

"There were a couple of messages from an unknown number. I could only get about four of the number."

"What was in the messages?"

"Well, one was asking the owner if they were going to be at 'over' … I'm guessing that's short for something. The other one said something like: 'Don't say anything about the other night'. I couldn't make out the rest."

"See if you can piece together anything more," he told her.

"I'll try, but it's pretty corrupted. That phone's been through the wringer, and that's saying something. The back was so full of rust it's as if someone dunked it in a pool or something."

"Or something," Jim said. "Thanks." He frowned at her. "Uh, you know, I didn't even get your name."

"It's Gaby," she said. She rolled her eyes. "Don't think I didn't get teased about that when I was in school."

He frowned at her. "Huh?"

"Gaby? Xena?" He still looked at her, confused. "TV show? Filmed right here in New Zealand? Ring any bells?"

He shook his head. "Sorry. Never saw it."

"Well, you might be the only one," she replied with a snort. "People went nuts over it when I was a kid."

"I guess," he said. "I'll let you get on with your work. Thanks Gaby."

Chapter Twenty-Seven

Matt Donaldson looked even more stressed than when she had last seen him when Amanda went to check on him at the school. Given the pressure he was under it was no surprise that he was in the office on a Saturday. He was surrounded by paperwork

"You look like you've got the weight of the world on your shoulders," Amanda observed from her position in the doorway.

He looked up and frowned at her. "Where the hell have you been?"

With the exception of the night before, Amanda wasn't sure she could explain the past few days and wasn't inclined to do so.

"You'll be happy to know the police have made an arrest," she said as she entered the office.

"One," he said morosely. "And not even the killer. Do you realise how much trouble this school is in? I have to face not only the school board at a special meeting tonight but now the Ministry is going to be all over this place next week."

"I thought they weren't sending the assessor in until next month?" she asked.

"They pushed up the timetable." He sighed. "Can you blame them? Two kids are dead and I failed to protect them."

"Matt, you can't blame yourself for this. Whatever has been going on at this school has been happening long before you took this job on. The fact is the board has been turning a blind eye to it for way too long. They've just swept it under the carpet hoping it goes away by itself. Things like this don't just go away. They grow and mutate, so by the time those idiots get off their butts and acknowledge the problem, it's too late."

"That's pretty much what your detective friend was saying." He sat back. His face was grey with exhaustion. He had dark circles under his eyes.

"You look like you haven't slept in days," Amanda said.

"I haven't." He looked at her. "You okay? I talked to your father the other night. He said you were pretty upset when you heard about Lori."

"I'm fine," she assured him. "I appreciate the concern though."

In spite of his mood he managed a small smile.

"I wasn't expecting to see you," he said.

"Well, I figured you'd want to hear what's been going on." She told him what she had learnt the night before from the bartender and what she had deduced.

"So what now?"

"I need to talk to Emma. Can you give me her details?"

"Shouldn't the police handle this?"

"If I'm right, Emma's too scared to talk to the police, otherwise they would have known about this before now."

Amanda had a theory that Emma's boyfriend had been killed as a message to her to keep her mouth shut. It was highly unlikely she remembered what had happened to her, since the cocktail of drugs known to be date-rape drugs left the victims with scattered memories but Mitch must have found out somehow.

She didn't explain this to Matt, despite the dubious look on his face.

"Matt, this might be the only way to get to the truth. About how Lori died and how Mitchell Cole died."

He stared at her. "You don't think Mitch's death was an accident?"

"No, I don't. But I can't prove that until I talk to Emma."

He still looked reluctant, but opened the lid of his laptop and tapped a few keys. He then grabbed a small square of paper from the holder on his desk and wrote something on it before holding it out to her. "Here," he said. "But you didn't get this from me."

Amanda glanced at it. The address was in Nelson Heights, just two blocks from the school.

"Thanks, Matt," she said. She turned to leave.

"Amanda …" She paused and looked at him. "Thank you. Not just for this, but … for understanding."

"It's like you said in the beginning Matt. You wanted to make a difference. Trust me, you are."

She left the school and headed to the address. The house was made of brick, much like the majority of the homes on the block. Amanda guessed that it was roughly fifteen years old, judging from the weathered look of the joinery.

A path made up of smooth clay bricks wound around from the garage to the front door. Several pairs of boots were scattered about the front porch as if the owners had just kicked them off and couldn't be bothered putting them away.

She rang the doorbell and waited, chewing on a nail. A woman opened the door. She was probably in her late thirties but time had not been kind to her face, which had more than a few wrinkles. Amanda grimaced at the cigarette in the corner of the woman's mouth.

"What?" the woman asked.

"Is Emma home?"

"Who're you?"

"A friend."

The woman didn't ask any more questions, but turned her head and yelled.

"Emma! Get your butt out here!"

Amanda waited for about a minute or two while the woman smoked and glared at her. Hostility came off the woman in waves.

Emma finally emerged, staring at Amanda.

"What do you ..."

"Emma, I need to talk to you. It's important."

The young redhead looked uneasy. Amanda studied her and the woman next to her. They didn't look at all alike.

"I'm not supposed to leave the house," Emma said. "My aunt ..."

"Just for a walk," Amanda said. "We won't go far."

Emma still looked worried, glancing at the older woman, who blew smoke in Amanda's face. Amanda coughed.

"Lady, give it a rest. You ever hear that second-hand smoke kills?"

"It's my house."

"Yeah, well it's my lungs and I like breathing."

Emma's aunt glared at her, taking the cigarette out of her mouth and pointing the end at her. Amanda returned the glare, waving her hand in front of her nose.

"You're rude, little girl."

"Right back at ya, and I'm not a little girl. Emma, come on. We need to talk. Unless you want ... your aunt, is it?" Emma nodded, looking uneasy. "Unless you want her to know about your extra-curricular activities." Amanda stared meaningfully at the girl.

The redheaded teen looked even more worried, while the woman looked confused. She didn't appear to understand the term.

Amanda pulled the girl's arm. Emma looked again at her aunt, who made no move to stop them.

"You shouldn't …" the teen began, but Amanda kept a firm grip on her arm, waiting until they were out of earshot of the house before speaking again.

"Emma, I know what happened to you. I also think I know why your boyfriend is dead."

"How can you … you don't know anything."

Amanda looked at her. Emma was pale. She seemed afraid.

"Emma, they tried to do the same thing to me."

Her face turned a ghostly white. She shook her head, murmuring something Amanda couldn't quite understand. They walked in silence for a few minutes before they passed a small reserve. There was a wooden bench beside a duck pond.

"Why are you here? Are you going to tell them?" Emma asked.

"Who? Kyle? For one thing, he's probably running from police and second, he's the one that tried to drug me."

Emma sighed, kicking her feet. She was shorter than Amanda by a few centimetres and fine-boned. She couldn't have fought off the attack even if she hadn't been drugged.

"I've been living with this for so long …"

"When did it happen?"

"A couple of weeks before you started at the school." Emma frowned. "Why would they do it to you? I saw you hanging around with them."

"It doesn't mean they considered me a friend. Emma, tell me what happened. What do you remember?"

She shook her head. "Nothing much. Lori used to talk to me at school and stuff. Mitch was always practicing with his team and didn't have much time for me, but she would come out and sit with me when I watched him play. One day she asked me if I wanted to go with her to this club. She said she didn't like going out alone, but she was going to meet some other kids there. Mitch went down south for the weekend and I had nothing else to do. My aunt was being a real pain so I went."

She continued on, telling Amanda that they'd gone to Rover. Lori had bought her a rum and coke. A little later Kyle and his friends had showed up. Emma had left her drink on the table to go to the bathroom. About half an hour later, she began feeling light-headed and disoriented.

"That's pretty much the last thing I remember until I woke up in the park," Emma said. "I felt so bad. My stomach hurt and everywhere else hurt. I didn't know where I was and I ran out into the road. This man in a taxi took me home."

"Why didn't you go to a hospital?" Amanda asked.

"I was scared. I didn't know what had happened to me and I was afraid my aunt would kill me if she found out I'd gone to a bar and was drinking."

"So then what happened?"

"I went to school and it was like Lori didn't want anything to do with me."

The more she listened to Emma's story, the more she realised Jim had been right. She <u>had</u> been naïve. Clearly Lori had not been an innocent victim in this after all.

"Emma, you need to talk to the police."

The girl shook her head. "I can't. You know what happened to Mitch. If you really think they killed him to keep me from telling someone then they succeeded."

Amanda placed a hand on her shoulder and shook her.

"Emma, I know you're scared, but two people are dead."

"They won't believe me," the girl insisted.

She had a good point, Amanda thought. Insofar as there was really no evidence of what had happened to the girl. She hadn't gone to the hospital that night and since the drugs didn't stay in the bloodstream, there was nothing to physically tie Kyle and the others to it. There was no proof Emma had been raped. Still, there had to be something her father could do.

"Look, I'm going to tell you the truth, okay, Emma? I'm not a student. I was sent to the school to get close to some of the troublemakers and help stop some of this."

The redhead stared at her. "Are you a cop?"

"No," she said, shaking her head. "But my dad is. If we go to him, he'll help you. I know he will."

Emma was silent, her expression thoughtful.

"Your dad will really help me?" she asked.

"Yes," she replied simply. She didn't want to make a promise she couldn't keep but she had faith in her dad. If anyone could help this poor girl, he could.

The redhead nodded. "Okay. Let's go."

Chapter Twenty-Eight

Jim stood outside the interview room where his boss was talking gently to the young girl. He'd known all along there had been something Emma wasn't telling him and now he knew what it was.

"Good work getting her to talk to us," he said quietly to Amanda.

She nodded, then bit her lip. "You will be able to help her, won't you? I mean, I know there's not enough evidence to prove ..."

For all their bickering, Jim knew Amanda was a girl who had a deeply compassionate nature. If the decision had been made on that alone, she would have made a good cop. Or a social worker, he thought.

"You let us worry about that," he said quietly. He pulled her aside. He could see she was stressed. "You okay?"

"No. I guess I'm just pulling my head out of the sand."

He nodded toward a small office. There was a couch where they could both sit comfortably. He guided her gently inside and closed the door.

"Sit down," he said. "I'm guessing you've been running around like a chicken with its head cut off."

"I just ... I thought Lori was innocent in all this, and now I realise she was part of the whole set-up."

"I'm sorry," he said. "I know you liked her."

"You were right. I was naïve."

He shook his head. "I had no right to say that. Yes, your instincts were wrong on Lori, but so what? Instinct isn't something that comes naturally, no matter what people say. It takes time to hone good instincts and believe me after five years I'm still trying."

"Part of me still wants to believe she didn't know, but now I realise after what happened that night that she did know. She was picking them and setting them up."

"Like lambs to the slaughter."

"Judas goat," Amanda said absently.

"I'm sorry?" he asked, not understanding the term.

"They used to use it in some farming practices. They'd train a goat to herd the cattle, or the sheep, usually so they could be rounded up and taken to the slaughterhouse. They were supposedly called Judas as a reference to Judas Iscariot, who was said to have betrayed Jesus Christ to the Romans and basically led him to his crucifixion."

He stared at her. Amanda was clearly a lot

smarter than he gave her credit for.

"Wow!" he said. "You're pretty well read for a …"

"Girl? Blonde?" she asked defensively, bristling visibly.

"Kid, I was going to say. Besides, I've never been one to think that girls can't do anything guys can, within reason. My stepmother is one of the smartest people I know. She also happens to be a natural blonde."

Amanda grinned suddenly. "Sorry. Guess that was my bad."

"Judging from the way you reacted, I would hazard a guess and say it happens a lot. People under-estimating you."

She shrugged. "I'm used to it. I, uh, got into an awful lot of trouble with my dad once because of a stunt I pulled in high school. He was not happy with me."

Jim snickered. "I bet." He looked at her. "So how did Mitch find out about what happened to her if Emma didn't tell him?"

Amanda looked uncomfortable. "Uh, porn," she said. "There's apparently a site where they allow anything to be uploaded and don't care about issues of consent."

Jim made a mental note to get a couple of constables to visit Mitch's mother and get his computer. He was sure Gaby could find the relevant files. It probably wouldn't get the site shut down, but it would still give them something.

Pete came in and grabbed a chair, turning it around and sitting down facing the back of it.

"Well, that little girl's a mess, but at least she's going to get the help she needs."

"Did she tell you everything?" Amanda asked.

Her father nodded. "Yes. Realistically, there isn't enough physical evidence to say that Emma was raped. If she had gone to hospital the night it happened, we might have been able to get something. Having said that, I've already sent a couple of guys to see Mrs Cole and get Mitch's computer. Even if the hard drive's been wiped, we should be able to recover the data."

"So what happens now?" Amanda asked.

"You've done your job, sweetheart. From what Matt's told me, the government assessor will take over. Whether he will be able to save his job I don't know. But this is where your job ends, honey."

"What about what happened to Lori?"

"Lori was still murdered, Amanda," Jim reminded her quietly. "That makes it our job."

"Well, look, I know it turns out I was wrong about Lori, but I still want to know what happens next."

"I'm sure your dad will keep you updated," Jim said, smiling at his boss.

"You did good, honey," her father told her. "Now go home and relax."

Amanda got up and hugged Pete. "Thanks, Daddy."

She went to the door, then turned to look at Jim.

"Thanks," she said. "You know, for a troglodyte, you're not bad." She smirked at him and left. Pete burst out laughing.

Jim shot his boss a look before dashing out the door to catch up with her. She had just reached the exit when he reached her. She looked at him, her eyes twinkling with laughter. He was suddenly at a loss for words, unable to think of anything cutting.

"What? No smart-assed remark? No pithy comeback?"

"Well, you know, you're no day at the beach either," he told her. "I will say this, since we're, you know, giving backhanded compliments ..." She was looking at him expectantly, as if saying: 'Do your worst'.

"You can't be that bad since your dad raised you."

"Is that the best you got?" she asked, raising an eyebrow.

He shrugged. "It's an off day. I'm sure I'll come up with something more cutting eventually."

"You wish," she retorted. "See you," she added, opening the door.

"Not if I see you first," he replied.

She scowled. "Grow up."

"You first!"

"Hey, technically I'm still a teenager. What's your excuse?"

"Do I need one around you?" he said.

"Oh my god! You always have to have the last word, don't you?"

"Oh you bet I do. If I let you keep nattering, I'd never get a word in edgewise."

"I take it back. You're not a troglodyte. You're a moron."

He had no comeback for that, damn it!

"Go home, Amanda."

She shot him one final glare before closing the door. Jim turned around to head back to his desk, not surprised to see his boss smirking at him. He glared at Pete.

"Don't. Say. A word."

The detective sergeant shrugged and walked off, chuckling. Jim stood shaking his head and sighing.

Jim knew there was little else he could do until they had more evidence so he decided to call it quits for the day. He went to the gym instead of home to work off some of his excess energy. When he got there, he found his friend Billy working out with the punching bag.

Jim grabbed a barbell and added some weights to it.

"How's it going with the case?" Billy asked.

His light grey t-shirt had turned dark with perspiration. Billy was lithe and fit with lean abdominal muscles. They had both begun going to their local health club while still in high school. Jim went because he'd been trying to get fit for the army and Billy so he could defend himself against the school bullies.

"We think we know who killed the girl but we haven't been able to arrest them yet. You got any more on that?"

Billy sniffed, wiping his face with his forearm.

"Not unless my boss has sent a report already. I mean, you know I only told you what I did because we're friends. It's going to be at least a couple weeks before we have anything we can say is conclusive."

"Yeah, guess so."

He chatted to Billy as they worked out. There was hardly anyone else exercising so they were left alone to talk. Jim told him as much as he could about what they suspected.

"So, you're saying teenagers are behind this?" Billy frowned. "I don't know, man. I mean, where did they get the stuff, for instance?"

Jim paused in lifting the barbell, frowning at his friend.

"What are you suggesting?"

"What I found isn't something you can get at the local market. I mean, it's not impossible, I suppose, but I kind of think there had to be someone older involved."

"Like a parent?" Jim asked. Or a teacher, he thought.

It made sense, he thought later, going over the conversation. GHB was usually bought over the Internet or cooked up in illegal labs. According to the records, a number of meth labs had been shut down by West Side police in the past few years. It was more than likely the drugs cooked up in those labs had been more than just meth.

He called in on his boss the next morning to discuss it over coffee. Pete Steele lived in a small two-bedroom house with a modern open-plan style kitchen-dining-living area. He had sold the three-bedroom house he had owned when Amanda moved into her own place. It certainly made it easier on the pocket, he'd told Jim, since it had reduced his mortgage payments considerably.

"Your friend makes a good point," the sergeant said. "And I think I know who you can talk to." He reached for a square slip of paper and a pen, writing down an address. "He's done time for drug dealing, among other things, but he's since given up on that. If anyone knows who might be dealing in these party drugs, he will."

"Thanks boss."

Deciding it was better to strike while the iron was hot, so to speak, Jim drove to a small house near the local beach community. It was isolated, with the nearest neighbour being at least half a kilometre away, but clearly the man preferred the isolation.

The house was down a long gravel driveway. Jim drove cautiously. While his police training had included driving at speed over any surface, he wasn't keen on risking his own vehicle unnecessarily. The so-called driveway was rough, with more than a few ruts in the gravel.

He studied the house as he pulled up at the end of the driveway. It had probably been built in the late 1960s. The boards appeared weather-beaten and could use a good re-paint. Jim observed that the window frames were not only slightly warped but the paint on them was badly chipped. A couple of the window panes were also broken. The yard itself was slightly overgrown with weeds mixed in with the grass.

A dog began barking loudly as he got out of the car. Before he'd even closed the door the dog had come to investigate, growling and snarling at what it considered to be an intruder. Jim could tell it was some kind of Rottweiler mix. Either way, he didn't trust it not to bite him if he moved.

"All right, all right. Ya dumb dog."

A man in bare feet walked over the grass, grinning at him.

"Don't worry. Her bark's worse than her bite."

"Oh, I'm not worried," Jim replied, eyeing the dog warily.

The man bent and grabbed the dog by the collar. He was short and skinny and hardly seemed much bigger than the dog. He looked up and smiled, showing gaps in his mouth. He was in his late fifties, with longish grey hair. He looked like someone who had lived through the hippy period and had never really left it behind.

"You'd be Jim, I s'pose."

Jim frowned at him. "How did you know?"

The man snorted. "Pete's a mate of mine." He smirked. "Well, if you could call a guy who arrested ya more times than ya can count a mate." The dog whined and tried to pull out of her master's grip.

"Let me get this mutt squared away and we can go talk in the house."

He didn't wait for an answer and pulled the dog away. Jim left the car and approached the house, hesitating a moment before stepping up onto the porch. Flies buzzed around the door where Jim could smell a very strong and unpleasant odour. He glanced around and spotted the source of the smell. There were several empty beer bottles sitting in a crate.

"Home brew," the man said behind Jim. "Well, come on in."

He followed his host inside the house, which also had a distinctive smell. Pot, he thought, recognising that burnt grass scent almost instantly.

His host didn't even have the grace to look guilty. "Pete's a good guy. Too straight, but then, he's a cop. Guess that means you are too, if he's your boss." The man peered at him, his eyes squinting. "Don't think I've seen you down station. You new?"

"Been there a couple of months," Jim told him.

"Ah, that explains it. Anyway, Pete knows I don't deal no more. Still smoke a bit now and then. Good for me arthritis."

The man's habit was probably not big enough for them to worry about or else his boss wouldn't have sent him here.

"By the way, name's Al. Pete told me what you're lookin' for. Truth is, I've been out of it a while but I still got contacts."

"He said you might have an idea who could be dealing these party drugs."

Al canted his head. "Well, guess that depends on your definition. Few years ago there was this outfit that dealt in these herbal things. Legal highs and all that. Supposed to be safe party drugs. Someone else got the idea to lace these herbal things with some of the not-so-legal shit and boom. Instant demand. Especially in the stupid little shits who like their kicks."

He paused, peering once again at Jim. "So Pete says some kids are using party drugs on little girls?" He shook his head and snorted in disgust. "Hell, I might not be kosher but I sure as hell don't go around doing little girls for kicks. That ain't right."

He sat down at a rickety table and opened up a laptop. "Got me some names. Figured it would help at least."

Jim looked at the screen, reading the names. "You know all these people?" he asked, noticing there were some feminine names in the list.

"A few. You hear about some in the joint."

Al had a list of about twenty names. He printed it off and handed it to Jim.

"Don't know how much help it'll be but sure hope you catch the little bastards. Like I said, I don't hold with what they're doing to those little girls. Bad business."

"Thanks Al," Jim replied.

He drove back into town, parking at the rear of the West Side station and going upstairs through the back entry to the bullpen. The office was quiet. Those who were rostered on for Sunday duty were probably out on calls.

Jim began searching the police database and cross-referencing them with Al's list. Nothing stood out until he got to the third to last name on the list and saw the man's photo.

"Oh no!"

Chapter Twenty-Nine

Amanda was usually an early riser. It was a habit she had developed in childhood, following her father who always had to be up early for duty at the station. Even on weekends. Sunday mornings were usually reserved for a workout at the gym followed by a slow stroll around the farmers' market.

A local business had gone bust years ago and the building was now used as a meeting hall for various community programmes. Amanda's aunt often played Bingo on Wednesday mornings. She was semi-retired but not yet at the mandatory retirement age. She enjoyed socialising with her fellow Bingo players.

The market was held in the parking area of the property. Some of the stalls were selling fruits and vegetables, while others sold books, toys, and second-hand collectables.

Her flatmate often went with her to the market, eager to find a bargain or two. She would pick up various knick-knacks and try to convince Amanda they needed it for the house, but it was mostly junk.

On those mornings a visit around the stalls felt like a marathon. Penny could be exhausting.

On this particular Sunday morning, Penny wasn't home. She had decided to go out clubbing the night before. She had tried to get Amanda to go with her, but Amanda had begged off, wanting to spend a night not doing anything that would require any major effort. It was not hard to guess Penny had met someone that night and decided to stay over.

Amanda had watched television most of the night, staying up late to watch a movie she had wanted to see at the cinema but had never got around to. Thanks to too many ad breaks, the movie had run over time and it was past midnight by the time she had gone to bed. Hence the late start. By the time she managed to get to the market, it was teeming with people.

She wandered around checking out the various stalls. Children were running around, making nuisances of themselves, while their parents were ignoring them. One little boy ran full tilt into Amanda, scowling at her when he fell over, as if she was in the wrong for being in his way. She glared back at him and skirted around him.

She was studying the concrete garden ornaments, thinking she should buy one for her father, who was a keen gardener, when she became aware of being watched. She looked around, trying to make it look as if she was looking for something else to buy and spotted the figure. He smiled at her.

She remembered him from the other night. DJ.

He fell into step with her. "Thought I saw you earlier," he commented. "How are you doing?"

"I'm doing okay," she said.

"No more getting lost down dark streets?" he asked.

She snickered. "Well, it would be pretty hard to get lost here, although in this crowd, I might have to rethink that."

She side-stepped to avoid a couple with a pushchair and an older couple trying to get past them.

"Come have a coffee with me," DJ said. "My place is just up the road."

"Thanks, but I really should …"

"I don't bite," he said, clearly trying to look offended that she would refuse to spend time with him. "Come on. It's just a coffee. I'm not asking you to have sex with me."

Amanda frowned. It was a strange thing to say and his tone seemed a little off. A couple nearby gave them odd looks, as if they had heard DJ's last words.

"I don't … know," she said, feeling suddenly a little uneasy. She started to edge toward a stall, wanting to get away from the man. He might have helped her the other night, but he had also got her almost blindingly drunk.

She still couldn't remember most of that night since the amount of alcohol she had drunk had affected her memory. However, she did recall that he had become quite pushy after she had tried to refuse a second glass of whiskey. The first one had gone straight to her head and she hadn't liked that lightheaded feeling. Normally she would limit herself to one or two bottles of an RTD or a glass of wine. Spirits had a far higher concentration of pure alcohol than anything else and if DJ had been correct about his friend's liquor, she would have got drunk on very little whiskey.

DJ grabbed her arm. It was obviously supposed to look like he was trying to keep her from tripping but the strong grip on her elbow told her he wasn't taking no for an answer. Not wanting to cause a scene, she let him pull her to the edge of the car park.

"You're a hard woman to pin down," he replied.

She stared at him, wondering what he meant by that. It caused her to wonder if what had happened the other night hadn't been an accidental meeting.

"Who are you?" she said. She tried to pull away, accidentally colliding with another couple trying to get into the market.

"Hey!" the woman said in protest.

Amanda shot her a desperate look before DJ pulled harder on her arm. She knew she had no choice but to go with him or else end up with a dislocated shoulder. There was no way she could fight him off with the crowds of people still trying to make their way into the market.

"Get off me!" she hissed.

He laughed at her. "Think these people care?

They'll just think you're having a domestic. Thing about people is, they don't want to get involved. Even if it's obvious a guy is beating the shit out of a woman."

"You're a freak!" she told him.

He laughed again. "A freak?"

Amanda felt someone collide with her, then a sudden impact on the back of her head. There was a brief pain accompanied by nausea before blackness took over.

She woke feeling disoriented, her head aching and her vision blurred. Her limbs seemed heavy and her whole body felt almost as if she were floating. It was a feeling similar to the time she had been taken for emergency surgery to remove a burst appendix. She had woken from the surgery barely able to keep her eyes open.

As she began to get her bearings, she realised she was lying on something firm but with soft cushioning. She sat up, ignoring the pounding in her head making the room spin.

She shook her head to clear her vision and saw DJ sitting across from her in an armchair. He appeared relaxed, as if he didn't have a care in the world.

What's wrong with this picture? she thought.

"Why did you bring me here?" she asked.

"Isn't it obvious?" he asked. "Of course, I don't exactly have the equipment here, so I've asked my friend to get it."

She stared at him. "What are you talking about?"

"Oh dear, and here I thought you were smart. I mean, I did wonder why Donaldson brought in outside help. Hate to say it, my dear, but you have absolutely no talent for acting."

Amanda guessed it was the blow to the back of her head which had made her a little slow on the uptake. A lot of things that had happened since Lori's murder were starting to make sense. Which also meant she was in serious trouble.

She opted for a bold approach, knowing she couldn't show any fear.

"Guess I won't need that Oscar speech I've been making up," she replied.

He laughed hollowly. She breathed deeply, hoping it would help her recover her senses before whatever he had planned came to fruition.

"Why me?" she asked.

He shrugged. "Well I do admit I didn't see you as the type. Not like the others. No, you strike me as pretty tough. Not as easily led."

"As girls like Emma, you mean?" she asked.

He gazed at her for a long moment, then nodded. "Exactly."

"So you and Kyle, and the other kids ..."

She thought it over. Someone had to have got the drugs. She doubted Kyle had been smart enough to source them, so they had obviously turned to someone who had the contacts.

What confused her was what had happened the other night. Why had he even bothered getting her drunk if he could have drugged her instead?

She asked him. He scowled at her in reply.

"Think if I'd had the stuff on me I would have wasted all that time getting you drunk? It was the best I could do with what little I had. Kyle was nowhere to be found and he was the only one I trusted with the damned supply. Even then you were still fighting me. I practically had to pour the drinks down your throat."

Good to know she still had her wits about her even when she was drunk.

"So … what? Are you saying running into me that night was a coincidence?"

"Call it a lucky break," he said with a smirk. "If that cop hadn't come along when he did, we wouldn't be having this conversation now would we?"

"You're an asshole!" she told him.

"Some would say that."

"If you think I'm gonna let you get your filthy hands on me, you've got another think coming!"

"You really think I care what you think?"

He got up from the chair and moved quickly to the couch. Amanda knew she only had one chance of fighting him off, hoping luck was with her. If Kyle, or whoever he had sent out came back, she would be outnumbered.

Her head was pounding and she felt as if she was going to be sick, but fear and a desperate desire to protect herself from further harm gave her what she needed to do so.

She struck out with a hard jab to the gut. DJ might have looked fit, but he clearly wasn't. He groaned, letting out a breath as if he was winded. Amanda had taken enough self-defence classes to know she had to follow through before he could recover. Using his body to steady herself, she got up, ignoring the sudden sensation of vertigo and kneed him in the groin, the blow landing just millimetres off centre.

Sufficiently recovered from the first blow and clearly angry, DJ grabbed her and shoved her hard, tripping her so she landed hard on the floor on her front. She rolled over quickly before he could get on top of her and grabbed his wrists, bringing her leg up and shoving her foot in his solar plexus. He was pushed back, landing hard on his tailbone, knocking over a small table on his way down. He groaned in pain.

She kicked up and out, flipping up to her feet, thankful for the years of exercise which had given her agility as well as flexibility. She stood over him, glaring.

"You bastard!" she said. "It's no wonder you had to knock me out. I wouldn't touch you if hell was frozen over, we were stuck on a desert island and you were the last man on Earth."

He was gasping for breath as he glared back at her. Amanda was about to deal the final blow when the front door opened with a loud crash.

Chapter Thirty

Jim studied the file on the man he suspected to have been behind the whole thing. He couldn't believe this was the same man who had been with Amanda the night she had got so drunk. It scared him more than he wanted to admit that if he hadn't happened on them when he had she could have ended up in the same mess as Emma. Or worse.

He accessed his files and discovered that DJ Walsh had taught physical education at a high school in Sydney before he'd been accused of molesting some of the female students. He'd protested his innocence, but Jim had his doubts.

Somehow the man had ended up working at Fraley High School. Either Donaldson had wanted to give him a second chance or Walsh had somehow managed to cover up his past.

Given that a former drug pusher had fingered the man as a possible dealer, Jim wondered if it was the latter. Especially as several girls had ended up being drugged and raped.

If that really was the case, then he needed to talk to Amanda and find out what she knew about DJ Walsh. He had an uneasy feeling in the pit of his stomach.

Jim called his boss and told him what he suspected. Pete sounded concerned but expressed his hope that Jim was somehow wrong.

"I'm not wrong," he told himself as he ran out to his car. "I've got a feeling ..."

He sped out of the carpark and down the road. Wanting to avoid being pulled over by the patrol and having to explain his actions, Jim kept the car to just under the speed limit, chafing at the restriction nonetheless.

As he reached the cul-de-sac where Amanda lived, he heard a call come over the radio. The operator was calling for units to check out a suspected domestic disturbance at the local market. Jim ignored the call and continued on to Amanda's place.

Her car wasn't parked in the driveway. However, Penny was just getting out of her car. She was wearing what appeared to Jim to be nightclubbing clothes. Short skirt and a sparkly top baring her midriff.

She looked at him and smiled.

"Well, hey there."

"Do you know where Amanda is?" he asked. "Her car's not in the driveway."

"I dunno. Probably the market. Hey, why don't you come inside and I'll make us some coffee."

"The market?" he repeated, his feeling of dread growing.

"Yeah, she goes every Sunday. She likes to look at the cheap knick-knacks. I go with her, to get fresh veges and stuff but ... hey!"

He ignored her shout, already back in his car and calling the call centre for details on the incident in the market.

"Any description of the people involved?"

"Only that there was a young woman, blonde and a man, also blonde, with a scar on one side of his face."

DJ, Jim thought. He thanked the operator and ended the call, placing another one immediately afterward. As he waited for the call to connect he turned the car around and drove back out to the street before turning on to the main road, driving at high speed.

"I need an address," he told the person at Central Communications. "DJ Walsh. Delta Juliet Whiskey Alpha ..."

"I have it," the operator replied, quickly reciting the address. "Do you need assistance, detective?"

"Send the nearest unit to the address," he ordered, pressing down on the accelerator and activating his siren. Most of the drivers on the road moved aside, but one idiot kept going, refusing to give way.

"Get out the way, idiot!" Jim shouted.

The driver continued to ignore him even as he signalled for the man to pull over. A passing patrol car stopped and did a u-turn. Jim took advantage of the gap in the opposing traffic and sped past the car in front, then indicated for the driver to pull over. The patrol car moved in behind. Jim stopped his own car and got out, moving cautiously. There were usually only two reasons why someone failed to give way to a police car with all emergency lights going. Either they were a complete ignoramus, or they were up to something. Jim's money was on the latter.

He approached the car warily. There had been a few incidents where a cop had been hurt because a driver had run them over trying to get away.

When he saw who was in the car, he wasn't surprised at their behaviour.

"Well, Kyle Harris. We've been looking for you."

A constable from the unit had also approached the car and overheard Jim.

"Damn, talk about lucky coincidence," she said. Jim smirked at Kyle, then looked at the officer.

"You can handle this from here, constable?"

The woman nodded. "Yes. Not a problem."

"Good. Thanks." He again smirked at Kyle. "I'll be seeing you later."

"Shoulda known you were a cop," Kyle replied with a pout. "Guess that means I was right about Mandy all along."

Jim wanted to stay and find out what Kyle had meant by that, but he had more pressing matters to attend to. He returned to his car and drove off at high speed.

He was at the address within minutes. The house looked roughly the same as every other house in the street. All of them had the appearance typical of former government housing. They were all basically the same design with only slight differences in the look of the exterior. This one was brick, with aluminium joinery. The front door had a screen door attached but the steel mesh had been ripped at some point.

As Jim pulled up his car behind a black kitted-out Subaru with a massive exhaust, a patrol car stopped on the kerb. He waved his hand, telling them to stay back until necessary.

He quietly approached the front windows and peered in. A couch partially blocked the view, but he could see movement inside. Then a loud crash could be heard accompanied by a loud groan.

Jim was up on the porch and kicking in the door before he'd even registered the thought. He entered the living room, only to be confronted by a pissed-off blonde, glaring down at a clearly winded DJ Walsh.

"Well," he said with a grin. "Guess you didn't need my help after all."

Amanda rolled her eyes flopped down on the couch. She watched as the two uniformed officers entered the house and dragged DJ to his feet.

Jim noticed she was more than a little shaky. While she tried to hide it, her hand was trembling.

As tough as she was, she had clearly been more than a little frightened by what had just happened.

"You okay?" he asked softly.

She shook her head. Jim knelt beside her and studied her. Now that the adrenaline of fighting off her attacker had passed, she seemed more than a little out of it. She rubbed the back of her neck and moaned.

"Amanda?"

"I don't feel so good," she murmured.

"Okay, that does it. I'm taking you to the hospital."

"I'm okay," she said. "It's just a headache."

"Did he hit you?" he asked.

"If not him, then someone else," she said. "I woke up here."

Which meant she'd lost consciousness at some point. He told her gently to stay where she was and went out to speak to the officers. He told them to let DJ cool off in the cells and he'd deal with him later.

Constable Linda Harvey, a woman who had joined the force after fifteen years in another career, looked worried.

"Isn't she Pete's daughter? She okay?"

"I think she may have a concussion," Jim said. "I'm not a doctor, but yeah, it looks like it. Can you call her dad? I'm going to take her to the hospital."

"Which one?" Linda asked.

"Think it's better if I take her to Central A&E," he told her.

He went back inside and saw Amanda was trying to curl up. He touched her shoulder.

"Come on," he said.

"Tired," she murmured.

"I know, but you have to get up." He helped her stand and let her lean on him. He walked slowly with her out of the house and helped her into the front seat of his car.

He kept his siren on as he drove at top speed to the central hospital, parking in the bay usually reserved for emergency vehicles. Amanda had been quiet the entire drive, barely awake enough to realise where they were. He helped her out of the car and walked with her inside.

"I need some help here," he called out.

A nurse came over. Jim showed her his police identification.

"I think she has a concussion." He told the nurse what Amanda had told him. The woman looked concerned and spoke to Amanda, who didn't respond.

"All right, let's get her to a bed."

Jim let her take over, getting Amanda to one of the beds in the emergency bay. Another nurse asked him to help her fill in the admission forms.

By the time he had given the staff all the information he had, Pete had arrived. He ran in, looking worried.

"Where is she?"

"She's being examined now by the doctor," Jim told him. "I heard them talking x-rays."

"How the hell did this happen?"

Jim related what he knew to his boss. Given how hard Amanda must have been hit, he was surprised she had had the presence of mind to fight back when DJ attacked her. Then again, this was Amanda. She was definitely her father's daughter.

Chapter Thirty-One

Amanda hated hospitals, but hated feeling unwell even more. After several hours of waiting, in between periods of being poked and prodded and asked various questions by the emergency staff, she was admitted to a ward. By then, her head was pounding so badly all she wanted to do was sleep.

Even that was something that eluded her. The nurse would wake her up every so often to check her obs. The situation was made even worse that she had to share the room with three other women, one of them snoring loud enough to wake the dead.

Consequently, she was in a bad mood by the next morning. Her head no longer hurt, but she was exhausted. She was anxious to be discharged, but ended up waiting until mid-morning when the doctor was doing his rounds.

"Well, how are you feeling this morning?" he asked.

"Box of fluffy ducks," she told him sarcastically. "When can I get out of here?"

"Amanda, you had a concussion resulting from a blow to the head. It's quite a serious injury."

"I know that," she exclaimed impatiently.

"I don't think you do," he replied. "Look, let me explain it this way. Your brain is like, well, you've eaten jelly before. Now imagine the jelly is in a container filled with fluid. The container gets bumped and moved around but the jelly remains intact because of that fluid."

She understood the seriousness of her injury but didn't like it being explained to her like she was a five-year-old.

"So what happens if the container receives a very hard impact? The jelly will slide back and forth against the edges of the container."

She nodded. "Which could change its consistency."

"In the case of your brain, the injury may cause bleeding, which in some cases is fatal. Your x-rays yesterday showed you received quite a blow to the head and your friend reported you were showing signs of drowsiness when he brought you in yesterday."

"He's a worrywart," she said. "Really, I feel fine."

The doctor nodded. "It's good that you feel fine. Your chart shows your blood pressure is normal and you responded well when the nurse checked your obs. That doesn't mean, however, that you shouldn't proceed with caution. I'm going to discharge you, but only if you have someone to look after you."

"Oh don't worry about that, doc," her father replied. "She's coming home with me for a couple of days."

Amanda looked at her father. Jim stood beside him, smirking. It was obvious he'd heard the conversation.

"So I'm a worrywart am I?" he asked as the doctor left the room, saying he would sign the form to discharge her.

"Yes," she told him smartly.

"Well, sue me for caring. If you'd seen the way you looked yesterday, you'd be worried too. You looked like crap."

"Gee, thanks," she replied.

An hour later found her settled on the couch at her father's house. She protested she was fine and just needed to get some sleep, but he didn't believe her.

Jim grabbed a chair from the dining table and sat astride it.

"So, thought you'd like to know we arrested Kyle yesterday. He admitted to being the one to hit you. As for your friend DJ ... the man wouldn't shut up. I know he was the one who got you drunk that night, by the way. So I take back what I said. Mostly. I still think you were irresponsible, but I understand now.

"Anyway, we've got him on charges including multiple rape and possession and manufacture of illegal narcotics."

She listened as he told her what else he'd learnt

through the interviews with DJ and Kyle.

Kyle had been planning on drugging Amanda and raping her, only Lori had stepped in. Her reasons for doing so hadn't been clear. According to Kyle, she had wanted out of the whole scheme after Mitchell Cole had been killed.

The scheme had been fairly simple. Lori would find the girls who seemed to be outsiders. Emma had been an error in judgement. Lori had known she had problems at home with an aunt who bordered on abusive, and a boyfriend who was more interested in playing sports than in actually spending time with her. Lori had mostly chosen girls who would have had no one to turn to afterwards, but Emma had chosen to go to DJ.

Lori had initially befriended Amanda thinking she would just be another one of the girls she usually chose, but Kyle had been suspicious from the start. He'd guessed that Amanda was a lot smarter than she pretended to be.

When one of the other boys involved in the scheme had seen her with Jim in the bar two days after she'd turned up at the school, it had just added to Kyle's suspicions. Amanda wondered aloud if there had been something in Jim's manner which had aroused those suspicions or if the boy had actually known he was a cop. It was something they wouldn't really know for sure.

"So Lori was killed because she wanted out? Not because she stopped them drugging me?"

Part of her was relieved that Lori's death wasn't technically her fault, while the other was sad that it had come to that.

"Why did they do it?"

"Greed," her father told her. "Plain and simple greed."

She frowned at him. While Jim had been bringing her up to speed, her father had been on the phone.

"That was Mark Gerraghty," he said. "It turns out that Kyle's father was the one who set up the website. Mr 'I'm a lawyer' thought he'd take advantage of what he saw were gaps in the law. He's been raking it in and sending the money overseas so we wouldn't catch it here. He's also the one who has been making noises with the school board, trying to cover up all the illegal activity going on at the school."

Jim snorted. "Typical."

Amanda looked at him and nodded her agreement.

"So what happens now?" she asked.

"We're trying to keep your involvement out of it so you won't have to testify in court. Put it this way, there's enough evidence to put these people away for a very long time and to shut down their operation. For good."

Good, she thought. At least a girl like Emma who found the courage to come forward would get some kind of justice.

Jim also explained that they were tracking down other girls featured on the website and making sure they received some help.

"So, now you've become a bigshot detective," Jim said, "you gonna apply again for police college?"

She thought about it for a second. "You know, I don't know about that. In spite of how things turned out, I liked what I was doing. Okay, maybe I didn't like getting knocked out and attacked by a serial rapist, but I think I'll keep working for Moody. Maybe now that I've solved my first case, he might even let me work on a few more."

Jim groaned. "God help us all!"

She grinned at her father, who winked at her, They both began laughing. Jim glanced at his boss, then back at her before joining in the laughter.

ABOUT THE AUTHOR

E.M. Richmond has been writing stories from her teenage years and could often be found scribbling ideas in a notebook.

She is an avid reader of the Spenser detective series by Robert B Parker which provided some of the inspiration for this novel. She professes a fondness for Nancy Drew mysteries and Trixie Belden. She also enjoys thrillers by Robert Ludlum and classic fiction by authors such as Alexandre Dumas.

E.M. Richmond lives in Palmerston North, New Zealand, where she grew up, although she has lived in other parts of the country.

She has a Bachelor of Arts in English and is also a qualified journalist.

Since leaving the newspaper profession behind she has continued honing her craft by writing fan fiction - stories using characters from various television shows. This has allowed her entry into worlds a kid raised in a lower middle-class, one-income family could only dream about.

OTHER BOOKS BY E M RICHMOND

Phoenix
Available on Amazon softcover and e-book

Abby was just a small-town reporter with a small-town future until a man imprisoned for a crime he did not commit begged for her help to prove his innocence. When the man is murdered, Abby realises there is much more to the man's story and it leads her down a dangerous and tragic path.

Abby must leave the past behind and become someone else to survive; to stop the man responsible for destroying her world.

Like the myth, she rose from the ashes to become Phoenix. But she may end up paying the ultimate price: her sanity or her life.

Michael Ryan's career as a police officer was all but over; then he was given the opportunity of a lifetime.

He chose to turn away from all he knew, giving up on love, until he met her.

Phoenix is determined to seduce Michael in order to infiltrate his world, but her attraction for him begins to get in the way.

They both have a lot of secrets. Will those secrets destroy their love or will they be able to find a way past the lies?

Can Michael save her … from herself?

Excerpt from Phoenix

Prologue

It was hot for late spring and the air was stifling. It was unusual weather for the time of year in a small town that sat in the shadow of snow-covered ranges.

All the houses along Market Street were quiet and dark for 11pm. There was the occasional flicker of light from a television screen in some of the residences, but few if any had the lights on in the rooms. No one wanted to add to the rising temperatures from the unexpected heat wave.

A woman walked along the street at what appeared to be a hurried pace. As she passed under a streetlight, her form cast a heavy shadow. The silhouette was lumpy, distorted, but it was not easily discernible if the woman was overweight for her height or if it was just a trick of the light.

The woman turned into the short driveway of a small house. Those who saw the house in daylight determined it was nothing special. Built in the early 1930s, it was in a bad state of disrepair. However, its tenant did not appear to be concerned by the sagging boards on the porch, or the peeling paint.

The tenant stepped up to the porch, turning her head to glance behind her. She paused on the step, her face, while still mostly in shadow, could just be seen by the light above her gateway.

She was 164cm in height and possibly close to forty kilograms overweight, her body, clothed in a short top and skirt exposing the flabby arms and chubby thighs which were a standard for women of her stature. Her age was indeterminate. She could be twenty-five or she could be thirty-five. Her weight certainly did not help. She was not well known to her neighbours. All most could say was that the woman kept to herself and was polite and quiet.

She took out a set of keys; the metal jangling in the quietness of the night and then inserted them in the Yale lock. Most would have cause to wonder why a woman alone would choose to live in a house so ramshackle and with just a cheap lock for security. This was a small town and many still believed it was safe enough to leave their doors unlocked and their windows wide open. Such was the mentality of small town New Zealand.

The door was opened and she stepped inside, over the rickety doorstep, her feet making a slight creak on a board that was bowed in the middle. She disappeared into the darkness of the small house, the door closing with a soft click behind her.

It could be ten seconds or twenty seconds later, but there came a flash and a loud explosion which shook the foundations of the house and several others on the street. As it was, the noise startled the neighbours out of their complacency, sending them running out of their houses, as if they were suddenly experiencing a magnitude seven earthquake. Startled though they were by the unexpectedness of the event, most could only stand and stare in helpless horror, like those known as rubberneckers, twisting their necks as they passed by a horrible accident scene. Not wanting to look, but still drawn to the tragedy.

Flames engulfed the building, licking hungrily at the dry, old wood. Those assembled continued to watch, speculating on the nature of this terror that had all too suddenly descended on their quiet, mundane lives. They all knew, without a shadow of a doubt, that had someone been inside that inferno, they would have instantly perished.

Some hours later, police and fire investigators were on site. A black BMW drove along the street, parking on the road behind a plainclothes police car. A man, aged somewhere in his mid-forties, with greying dark hair got out of the car. He was tall about one point eight metres, with a slim, athletic build. He was wearing a charcoal grey suit which marked him as someone official.

He walked along the street to the front of the ruin, observing a young man writing furiously in a notepad while talking to one of the uniformed officers. He continued on past, approaching a man in the dark blue uniform jacket of the fire service.

"Can I help you?" the investigator asked, sucking on the end of a cigarette.

The man pulled out a wallet, flipping it open to show some identification. The fire investigator nodded.

"What have you found?" the man asked.

"Cause is undetermined."

"Body?"

"Not yet, but that means nothing. It depends on whether the occupant was at ground zero at the time of the explosion. There may be nothing to find."

"How sure are you?"

The investigator's grin was sickly.

"About as sure as I am of winning Lotto this weekend."

"I'd like to see inside."

The fire investigator waved a hand, gesturing toward the blackened porch. "Be my guest."

The man walked inside, picking his way through the ashes, the piles of charred wood, his shoes crunching on broken and melted bits of glass. His gaze fell on a small spot of colour in the destruction and he walked over to it, digging it out. It was a photograph, its edges charred, the surface bubbled from the heat. It was of a young woman and an older couple. The women looked similar. Mother and daughter, he assumed.

Turning, he walked out again, nodding to Coleman, and returning to his car.

Reporter missing after late night inferno –
The Times, November 20

It is with great shock and sadness that we here at The Times must report the possible death of one of our own.

Abigail Smith, 25, a reporter for the last two years at The Times, is missing, believed dead after her house was destroyed in a massive explosion which could be heard for several kilometres.

Police and fire investigators have still to determine the cause of the explosion, which occurred around 11pm yesterday.

It was believed Ms Smith had only just arrived home after working late night at this newspaper.

Fire investigator Bill Coleman said it will take several days for the cause of the explosion to be discovered.

He said the forensics team will be sifting through the damage in the hope of picking up clues.

Senior Sergeant Mark Donohue said there was always a possibility that Ms Smith was still alive, she could be badly injured and he is hoping she will be found.

He said police were very familiar with Ms Smith due to her line of work.

"We have known Abby for two years and we have always found her to be a personable young woman.

"She's quiet, but she has always shown remarkable integrity for someone so young.

"Should it be determined that someone has deliberately done this, believe me, we will be leaving no stone unturned to discover who is responsible for such a heinous deed to a lovely girl."

Ms Smith recently suffered two very tragic losses when her parents were killed in a boating accident eight weeks ago.

Her partner, Scott Jensen, was also killed in a car accident less than a month ago.

Police are asking for anyone with any information on Ms Smith's whereabouts to contact them urgently.

Max Sutton put down the newspaper with a sigh, combing his fingers through his greying hair. He took his i-phone from the desk and accessed his email.

Need to meet. ASAP. Usual place.

The message came back within the hour.

On my way.

Max waited. The warehouse where he met his contact looked abandoned from the outside. It had been an old clothing factory once upon a time, but years of economic yo-yoing had left the previous owners with no choice but to abandon it.

"Max."

He turned, looking at the man with dark blonde hair. He had no idea where his friend had come from and didn't ask.

"What's going on?" Michael Ryan asked.

Max showed him the paper. Michael read it thoroughly.

"They got a cause yet?"

"No. Coleman made his best guess that it was arson. The cops are clueless."

"They would be. Where is she now?"

"We don't know. She hasn't shown up at the local hospital and none of her friends have heard from her."

"She could be dead," Michael said.

"I doubt it," Max told him.

"We need to find her."

"Girl may not want to be found." He looked at his friend. Michael had that look. "Mike, don't do it. She's not worth blowing this for."

Michael shook his head. "No one cared enough to stop this before it was too late. Someone has to care. Someone has to."

"And I'm not about to let you jeopardise everything we've spent the last six months setting up. We must continue with the operation as planned."

"She knows ..."

"She doesn't know everything."

Letting Go

On Amazon softcover and e-book

A call in the middle of the night wakes Janet with some bad news. Her best friend has killed herself. Janet looks for answers as she slowly deals with her grief through some journals left behind and discovers her friend has hidden a painful secret.

Her own journey of discovery begins to interfere with her personal life until she almost reaches breaking point. She has help from a man who knew her friend, knew her and cared for her, but never had the chance to tell her. As the pair grow closer, Janet begins to let go, finding hope and love.

This is a story which delves into the consequences of mental illness and suicide. It contains themes of abuse, both physical and emotional, but is ultimately a story of finding the strength to let go. Of hope.

Excerpt from Letting Go

Chapter One

The harsh bell of the telephone ringing outside my door woke me from a deep sleep. Still groggy, I was tempted to roll over and clap the pillow over my head to muffle the sound until it started to register that it was still dark in the room, which meant it wasn't even close to morning.

Groaning, I rolled onto my side as the ringing became almost insistent, echoing in my ears. I squinted at the numbers on my digital clock, barely able to make them out. Three am, or close enough.

When I was growing up, there had always been a strict rule that no family or friends were allowed to call after nine. Up until I was seven years old, I grew up on a working dairy farm which was now run by my father. Dad was used to retiring around ten o'clock, so he could be up at five the next morning ready for the milking. So if anyone called in the middle of the night, it had to be a dire emergency.

I remembered there was one incident where someone kept calling at two o'clock in the morning; once a week, without fail, for about six weeks. We never knew who it was as the person never spoke, according to my dad. He eventually got onto the phone company and got them to track the calls, but he was so mad.

I kind of enforced that rule with my own friends. I'd had flatmates who had people ringing at all hours and I finally had to put my foot down with them, telling them in no uncertain terms that it better be an emergency or else the phone was getting shut off at night.

So if someone was calling me at three o'clock in the morning, there had to be something wrong.

The phone was still ringing. Only seconds had passed but with my mind still half asleep, it felt like minutes. I stumbled out of bed, tripping over my slippers as I staggered to the bedroom door before opening it and grabbing the phone which stood on a table in the hallway. It was a fixed set and the cord tended to tangle. The sound of the ringing cut out as I picked it up and for a moment I thought I had lost the call.

"Hello?" My voice was still croaky with sleep. I'd always felt like a total dork when it did that as it sounded weird to my ears.

I thought the person had hung up after having waited for so long, as there was no reply on the other end, yet I could hear something. Like snuffling, or little whimpers.

"Hello," I said again, knowing it sounded kind of redundant, but really, I didn't know anyone who could think clearly at that time of morning, especially when they'd been woken up from a deep sleep. I cleared my throat and tried again. "Are you there?"

The sounds increased in frequency and volume. I was going to say 'hello' a third time when a female voice spoke in a hesitant tone.

"Janet?"

I frowned. I thought I knew the voice, but they were sobbing in-between breaths and I couldn't quite tell who they were.

"Yes?" I grimaced. I didn't know why, but it just sounded like a stupid thing to say.

There were more sobs as if she was struggling to get the words out. I held on, trying not to make any impatient sounds.

"It's Callie. She ... she ..."

She what? I thought.

The voice broke and the person on the other end began sobbing as if her heart was broken. I began to get a sick feeling in the pit of my stomach and a cold sweat broke out on my forehead. I took a deep breath, trying to calm myself.

"What happened to Callie?"

"She ... I ..."

I remembered reading about a guy who worked for emergency services in America who told a hysterical girl to stop whining while she was trying to get help for her dying relative. At the time I thought that was quite a rude thing to say, but it had occurred to me that he'd probably been trying to get her to calm down but it had just come out wrong. With that in mind, I knew if I huffed or made any sounds of impatience, it would just make it that much more difficult for the girl on the other end of the phone.

I waited. She was clearly taking deep breaths, trying to calm herself, but the crying didn't stop.

"What's happened?" I repeated.

"She's … she's dead, Janet."

I'd flown from Wellington, our capital city, to Sydney in Australia for a work conference one year. The flight had been in rough weather and there was a lot of turbulence. There had been one point where I'd almost felt the contents of my stomach come back up to meet me as the plane dropped, hitting a downdraft. That was exactly the way my stomach felt as I heard those words.

"What?" I asked in disbelief.

"I came home and she was … she was … I called the ambulance but by the time they got her to the hospital it was too late."

Now I knew who the caller was. Her flatmate, Susan. They'd been living in the same house for the past few years. I'd met Susan when I'd gone to help Callie move in and we hadn't got along very well. It wasn't that I disliked Susan. I just couldn't understand why Callie would move in with a girl who was everything she wasn't.

It seemed odd that I had been the first person Susan had thought of to call with this news, thinking that maybe she should have called Callie's parents first, but I figured that sometimes people just didn't think rationally when things like this occurred.

Callie was my best friend, and now she was gone. What had happened?

"Susan, have you called her parents?" I asked, trying to figure out her thought processes. It wasn't to say that Susan was unintelligent, but even though we'd had little to do with each other, my opinion of her wasn't exactly favourable.

Susan sounded much calmer as she replied, as if she was over the hardest part.

"I … I thought it would be better coming from you," she replied.

I nodded, knowing how redundant it was, since she couldn't see me. I supposed she was right. It would be better coming from me.

"You're probably right." I took a deep breath. A million questions had run through my brain and as hard as it was learning the news, there was one more thing I needed to know. "Susan, what happened?"

"She killed herself Janet."

If it had been an accident, or natural causes, I think I could have handled it better. As it was, I nearly dropped the phone in shock. I'd known Callie had a few problems, especially with depression, but the thought that she would do something like this ...

I inhaled and exhaled slowly for a few breaths to calm myself before I spoke again.

"Susan, I need to call Mr and Mrs James. Will you be okay?"

"When can you get here?" she asked, as if it was a given that I would just get in the car and start driving at three in the morning.

"I need to make a couple of calls first, but I should be there about ten-ish."

That gave me roughly six and a half hours to get myself organised and drive from my place to hers. Callie lived ... had lived in Auckland, which was roughly four hundred kilometres away from the Hawkes' Bay, a small province on the east coast of the North Island of New Zealand. We had never cared about the distance, talking on the phone every few weeks or video calling each other on Skype. We'd been friends nearly all our lives and we'd never let anything change our friendship.

Now everything had changed.

I said goodbye to Susan after making sure she would be all right, then pressed the disconnect button on the phone, preparing to dial the number for Callie's parents.

I couldn't see the buttons on the handset. Rolling my eyes at the inanity of it, I reached over and switched on the light in the hallway, blinking rapidly at the sudden brightness. I began dialling.

I glanced over at the clock on the wall as I waited for the phone on the other end to be picked up. It was three thirty.

"Hello?"

Clearly the phone was right next to the bed as it was picked up fairly quickly. However, the voice on the phone sounded just as addled as I had been when I'd first picked up Susan's call. I wanted to give her a few seconds to adjust but she might have hung up the phone again if I didn't answer.

I was surprised at how calm I was as I spoke to Marion.

"It's Janet. I ... Marion, it's Callie. She ..." I grimaced. How could I tell her mother that her only daughter had killed herself? "She's passed away."

It sounded so ordinary to describe something so terrible, but I couldn't tell her the truth. It was hard enough for me to deal with it.

There was silence on the other end, then a loud clang which hurt like hell as the noise went through my head. I heard Marion speaking to her husband Richard but I couldn't make out what she was saying. She seemed almost unnervingly calm as she spoke.

"I'm sorry," she said. "I dropped the phone. What happened?"

"I'm not sure of all the details. Susan wants me to come up. I don't think she knows what to do."

"Janet, what are you not telling me?"

"I'm so sorry, Marion," I said, feeling the lump in my throat. I could feel the tears threatening but I continued to fight them. She deserved to know the truth, but if I told her I would have to face the stark reality. My best friend had killed herself.

I didn't want this to be real.

Second Time Around

Available on Amazon softcover and e-book

Georgia Hayden is an established business journalist for a major media company in Auckland, New Zealand. Travelling back from a business conference, she spots an old friend. When Georgia is asked to interview the old friend, he is reluctant.

Business mogul Quinn Masters lost his wife thirteen years ago and left New Zealand for the UK, hoping to raise his daughter away from the attention of the media. When he returns home after twelve years, he knows there will be some speculation but still wants to protect his daughter.

Then Georgia convinces him to do the interview. Neither of them expect to discover a mutual attraction.

They're both gun shy, for their own reasons. If they can just find a way to get past those issues, they may find love is indeed lovelier the second time around.

Chapter One

Georgia Hayden sighed wearily as she stared out through the window of the Boeing 747, her head so close it was almost touching the pane. Not that there was anything to see, she thought, but it provided a convenient distraction from the monotonous drone within the cabin and allowed her to ignore any attempts by her seatmates to engage her in conversation. It seemed it was a reasonably sunny day in New Zealand, although Georgia, at twenty-eight, had been around long enough to know that it could be sunny weather in one place and raining less than one hundred kilometres away. Such was the nature of the country's unpredictable climate, especially in late autumn.

The plane dipped and shook a little, eliciting gasps from some of the less seasoned travellers who clearly weren't used to the constant dip and roll motion when a plane hit a downdraft. Georgia was used to the turbulence, having once been in a plane forced to fly around a lightning storm. They'd been lucky then not to have been hit by the lightning, skirting the worst of the storm, although it had caused an hour delay in the flight. While she didn't mind flying, the long flights being stuck in claustrophobic conditions could get tedious after a time.

She sighed heavily, her breath misting on the window. It had been an extremely long and exhausting flight. It hadn't helped that all the seats had been booked, so it was a full plane from Sydney to home. What had made it even more exhausting was the fact that she had basically been in the air for close on twenty-four hours, not counting the delays and the layovers.

Georgia had spent the last ten days in New York on a conference. Ten days of meetings, seminars and barely time for her to eat dinner and fall into bed each night. She'd left New York via JFK international airport early in the morning, eastern standard time and flown to Los Angeles where she had been forced to wait another five hours before her plane to Sydney boarded. Taking into account the three-hour time difference between the east coast and the west coast and it was little wonder she was tired. She had barely been able to doze on the journey over the Pacific.

More than fourteen hours later, early morning fog had forced the pilot to divert the plane to Brisbane where they'd had to wait on the tarmac for another hour for the weather to change before they could return to Sydney, adding another two hours which would have been completely unnecessary if they had been able to get in to Australia just an hour later.

Three hours after her arrival in Sydney, Georgia had boarded the plane for home, only to be sat next to what had to be the most irritating man in creation.

Her seat mate had begun flirting with her the moment she had sat down and Georgia was too tired to even put him in his place. She had hoped by flying business class that it would prevent such an occurrence, but clearly not. She had been squashed against the window as the man, while not necessarily overweight, but definitely big in stature, had taken up his seat and encroached on more than a few centimetres of hers. Either he was really bad at flirting or his knee bumps had been accidental, but Georgia didn't think so.

She'd finally had to turn the full force, or as much as she could muster, of a glare on the man and tell him to knock it off.

"Listen, I have spent most of the last day and a half in a poor excuse for a flying coffin and I am tired and bitchy. Leave me alone!"

The man had seemed taken aback, staring back at her as if she had two heads or something.

If she hadn't been so tired, she would have considered the man good-looking with his short, spiky blonde hair and intense hazel-eyed gaze. Except for the fact that he had an arrogant, look down his nose smirk.

As tired as she was, she had been well aware of the way the man had been leering at her, trying to see down her top. Georgia had put on a cream-coloured t-shirt and black tailored pants when she had dressed for the flight, knowing she would have to wear the outfit for two days and wanting to be comfortable. The top didn't show any cleavage, but clearly that hadn't stopped her companion, who had continued to ogle her despite her snapping at him.

It was sexual harassment of the worst kind and if she had had more energy, she would have asked the flight attendant to see if she could move to another seat or get him to move, but she had figured it was only for three hours, give or take, and she could put up with it.

"Ladies and gentlemen, we will be landing shortly at Auckland International Airport. Local time is three-thirty pm and the temperature is a balmy ten degrees Celsius." The flight attendant prattled on, giving what sounded to her like some kind of script they often used for tourists.

Georgia rolled her eyes at the comment on the temperature. Balmy, she snorted to herself. I'll give him balmy. Ten degrees in the city was more likely to be about five degrees or less.

She glanced at her watch, making sure it was adjusted to local time. The announcement had advised the landing would be in approximately twenty minutes. Georgia calculated it would be another hour after landing, figuring it would take that long to get through customs, before she could meet her friends, who had told her they would pick her up from the airport and drive her home. Great, she thought with another heavy sigh. She felt she hadn't slept much at all during the last twenty-four hours and she was so tired she didn't think she'd be able to hold out another hour.

"As we start our descent, please make sure your seat backs and tray tables are in their full upright position. Make sure your seat belt is securely fastened and all carry-on luggage is stowed underneath the seat in front of you or in the overhead bins. Thank you."

The intercom clicked off and passengers began moving about, putting away various items. Georgia leaned forward to slip her bag under the seat in front of her, putting her tray table away. As she did so, her neighbour leaned over to adjust the back of her seat.

"Let me help you with that," he said, a smarmy expression on his face.

She scowled at him. Really? Did she look like she couldn't fix a seat all by herself? He continued to ogle her, making her feel distinctly uncomfortable. His hand brushed her breast. Georgia was sure it had been deliberate but had no doubt he would protest and tell her it had been purely by accident.

"You know, if you're free later ..." he began, smiling at her in a way she guessed was supposed to be friendly. Again, it had the opposite effect. While it wasn't creepy, it was still unwelcome.

God, she thought. Did this guy never give up?

"Actually," she said, "I won't be. My family is meeting me."

The man glanced down at her left hand. Georgia chewed her lip. She'd always had slim hands with long, delicate fingers. Her nails, however, seemed to always be on the critical list. Her best friend was forever trying to get her to get a full manicure, but Georgia just didn't see the point. In her line of work, especially with her constant typing on keyboards, a manicure would last five minutes, if that.

"I don't see a ring," her seatmate hinted.

"It's the twenty-first century," she told him, wondering why she was even engaging in any kind of conversation with him. "Not everyone needs a ring."

She glanced down at her ring finger. There had once been a slight tan line from her wedding band, but it had been more than two years since she'd taken off that ring and her skin was now a light brown which was quickly fading to her usual pale. Georgia had always had fair skin which never seemed to really tan in summer. The darkest she had ever been able to achieve was a sort of olive brown.

Her parents had been worried when she had announced she was getting married, just four months after she had begun dating her fiancé, suggesting she was too young at twenty-three to know what she wanted, but Georgia had thought she was in love and that it would last forever.

Of course, she hadn't counted on her ex-husband changing the moment they'd got married, or the fact that she had caught him with another woman, she thought darkly. The experience had made her a little bitter toward men and even more wary of them, especially when they blatantly flirted with her.

Even as the flight attendants began bustling about, moving up and down the aisle to check everyone had followed the pre-landing procedure, her neighbour refused to be deterred, keeping up a steady stream of chit chat. Georgia found herself sighing once more, resigned to being stuck in this predicament until the plane landed.

The man irritated her no end. He'd kept telling her she was beautiful. Sexy, even. Georgia had always had trouble believing that, especially in high school. She'd once had a crush on the boy who was now her best friend's husband, although like any teenage girl, her crushes tended to last only as long as the next pin-up came along. It was a good thing she had realised a long time ago that it really had been infatuation, otherwise she could never have handled her two best friends getting married and starting a family together.

She had put those years of insecurity behind her, choosing instead to focus on her talents as a writer. She had dated a couple of guys in high school, mostly boys her friend Lacey had hooked her up with so they could double-date with Lacey's now-husband Adam, then had had a fairly serious boyfriend at university. After the break-up of her marriage, however, Georgia had decided she didn't need a man to make her complete. She had enough to worry about with her job and her ...

She felt the plane begin to descend and her ears blocked up, muffling out most of the noise. She quickly pulled out a hard boiled sweet from her jacket pocket, tearing the cellophane packet, and popped it in her mouth. She'd been told that it usually helped unblock the ears, as it produced saliva, which made her swallow. Maybe it was an old wives' tale, she thought, but it was better than nothing.

The plane descended and hit the tarmac with a jolt, making a sharp turn a few seconds later that threw her up against her companion. Great, she thought. Just what I need.

The man again smirked at her, putting his hand on her knee. She was expecting him to feed her some line about Prince Charming, or whatever, but when she turned a vicious glare on him, he quickly backed off, removing his hand. Good, she thought, because any more of that and I'll break your finger.

She was more than capable. Her ex had known a little karate and had taught her some self-defence moves. While she hadn't exactly had to use them, she still practiced them now and again, preferring to keep up her fitness. Just in case.

Another voice, which she assumed was the head flight attendant, could be heard over the intercom.

"Welcome to Auckland International Airport. For your safety and comfort, please remain seated until the captain turns off the seat belt sign. At this time, you may use your cellular phones if you wish.

"Please check around your seat for any personal belongings you may have brought on board with you and please use caution when opening the overhead bins, as some articles may have shifted around during the flight.

"If you require assistance, please remain in your seat until all other passengers have deplaned. One of our crew members will then be happy to assist you. On behalf of Air New Zealand and our crew, I'd like to thank you for joining us on this trip. For those who are returning home from travels, we hope to see you again in the near future. For those visiting New Zealand, enjoy your stay."

There was a ding and the light indicating all passengers needed to wear their seatbelts switched off. Georgia quickly pulled at her seatbelt, tossing it so the metal of the buckle clanged against the arm of her seat and got to her feet to manoeuvre herself past her two seatmates and grab her laptop and carry on case from the overhead bin.

Ignoring the passengers still gathering their own carry-ons beside her, she strode purposefully and swiftly down the aisle toward the main door, which the flight attendant had just barely managed to open.

"Have a great day, ma'am," the man said, smiling at her.

Georgia just strode past him, knowing it was rude, but she didn't care. Was too tired to care and too anxious to escape.

She pulled her case behind her as she made her way down to the customs area of Auckland International Airport. She caught a glimpse of her reflection in one of the glass panes and scowled at it. She looked a mess. Her blonde hair looked as if, as her mother would say, she had been dragged through a gorse bush backwards. It was a mess of tangles, despite being short enough to be almost a boy cut. Her roots had started to show. While Georgia was naturally blonde, her natural colour was more a mousy blonde and she'd had it lightened.

Her eyes, normally a blue-green, had turned almost a sea green, reflecting her exhaustion. She blinked a few times, hoping to ease the irritation from the dryness caused by the long flights.

She thought about the trip as she continued along the long corridor, digging in her handbag for her passport and declaration form. A pamphlet had stuck to the back of her passport and she studied it for a moment. It was just a little tourism brochure she had picked up in the hotel in New York on the Empire State Building, claiming the building, once the tallest in the city, was where the 'real magic' of New York could be found. Georgia would have loved to have had time to do some sightseeing while in the city the Americans liked to call the Big Apple, but there hadn't been any time between meetings and writing up her reports to send home.

She hated the business trips sometimes, but they were a necessary evil. It was the price she paid for having become one of the top business reporters in the country.

Georgia had always wanted to be a reporter, from the moment her high school English teacher had suggested it would be a good career for her. She had devoted most of her time to fulfilling that ambition, begging the editor of the local newspaper for a job during the summer, even if it had meant fetching coffee, before going to university.

By the time she had graduated with her journalism degree, there was talk in the industry of print journalism dying a slow death. Online was the only way up, or so she was told. Georgia had taken that on board, absorbing every bit of information she could to learn what it would take to be the best in her field, even to the point of taking a few computer classes to ensure she had fairly extensive knowledge on the latest technology.

It had taken years of hard work and a lot of articles which amounted to lightweight stories, but it had been worth it.

Now she felt she had earned her reputation, and deserved the accolades that came with it, even if it did mean she had to take the occasional press junket. If only they left her time to do a little sightseeing, she might enjoy them more, she thought. Still, there were some concessions, since some of the trips had included openings of luxury hotel resorts.

Georgia continued moving, quickly joining the line of her fellow countrymen returning home from their own trips, their hands full with a variety of bags. Young children stood by their parents, clearly too tired to do anything except complain endlessly about the line.

She didn't envy the passengers from other countries who had an even longer line to get through customs. It was nowhere near as bad as it had been in Los Angeles when she had first arrived in the United States, where it had taken two hours to get through their border control. It was a pity her bosses hadn't considered diverting through San Francisco instead, as one of the American passengers had told her processing there was much quicker than LAX.

It was understandable that they had become stricter with their security measures, especially since 9/11. Knowing that didn't make it any less tedious, however.

She dug in her handbag for her phone to switch it on, anxious in case it took a little longer for her to get through customs and not wanting her friends to worry. Just as she turned back to the line, she was nudged from behind. It was her nemesis.

"You dropped this," he said, handing her a small snapshot of a little boy with fair hair and a dimpled smile.

Georgia frowned at it, then hastily thrust it back in her bag.

"Cute kid," the man said. She recalled he had told her his name when they'd first sat down, but her weary mind couldn't remember it. He continued to gaze curiously at her, his eyes dropping as if he was looking her up and down. Georgia fought to suppress a shudder.

"Yours?" he enquired.

"Yes," she replied shortly. Not that it was any of his business. She began to move away, but he touched her arm, stopping short of actually grasping her elbow.

"Listen, I was wondering … you want to go for a drink?"

She shot him an 'are you kidding'? look.

"My family's meeting me," she said, aware that she was repeating herself, but he just didn't seem to be getting the message that she wasn't interested.

"Hubby?"

She pointedly ignored him, moving up as the family in front of her also moved up. She let her attention wander, looking around at the various people in line.

Her gaze fell on a tall man with dark brown hair and olive skin talking to one of the customs officers. Beside him stood a girl with reddish blonde hair. She was in her early teens, but clearly tall for her age, as she came up to just a few centimetres short of her father's shoulder. At least, Georgia assumed he was the girl's father. She frowned as she studied his profile. The man seemed sort of familiar.

"Huh," she said to herself, watching as the man took his now stamped passport, along with the teenage girl's and stepped through the security area.

Georgia continued to stare, open-mouthed, a name suddenly springing to mind. It couldn't be! she thought, startled.

He must have felt the weight of her stare because he looked around. Georgia caught a glimpse of intense blue eyes and her heart skipped a beat.

Quinn Masters!

"Ma'am?"

Georgia returned her attention to the line of security booths in front of her and stepped up to the customs officer. He wasted no time in checking her passport and declaration and sent her through.

She continued to look for the man she thought was Quinn, craning her neck and standing on her toes trying to see above the people milling about, but couldn't see where he went. Sighing, she made her way through to the baggage claim area, grabbing her suitcase from the carousel as soon as she spotted it, before heading for the booths where some passengers were already getting their luggage checked.

She was quickly waved through, the officers satisfied she was not carrying any kind of contraband. Quinn was nowhere in sight when she finally reached the arrivals area.

In spite of her exhaustion, she smiled when she spotted the tall, dark-haired man standing beside her best friend, Lacey Johnson-Granger. They grinned at her. The couple's two-year-old son, JJ, began bouncing up and down, excited to see her. His five-month-old sister curled in her father's arms, her face hidden in his chest, the only part Georgia could see was her dark, curly hair.

Lacey wrapped her in a welcoming embrace.

"Hey kiddo," she said affectionately.

Georgia almost scoffed at her friend. Lacey was only a few months older than her but still called her kiddo as if the gap was even wider.

"How was the flight?" Adam asked.

Georgia groaned. "Don't ask," she said, offering her friend a weak smile.

The three of them had become known as the terrible trio in high school. Georgia was never sure who was really the instigator of all the pranks they had pulled on their classmates. Probably Lacey, she thought. They had never been mean-spirited and even their teachers hadn't had the heart to give them detention. They had been well-liked by everyone at the school, although Georgia had always been considered the more serious member of the trio. Still, they'd had some good times together.

She looked her friends over, smiling fondly at the memory. When she'd realised Adam and Lacey had the same wicked sense of humour, despite the way the continually bickered, she knew they were meant for each other. It had taken a year or two for them to get over themselves long enough to actually see it, but they had been together since their last year of school.

Lacey tossed her head, her long chocolate brown tresses bouncing. The woman was tall with a slender frame and long, long legs. She had what Georgia considered to be the kind of bone structure most models would kill for, but Lacey had never been interested in becoming a model.

Her hazel eyes sparkled as she looked her friend over.

"So, hate to say it, kiddo, but you look like hell."

Georgia snorted at her best friend. "Gee, thanks. I really needed to hear that."

"Seriously, you do. You've got more baggage than an airport under your eyes. Did you get any sleep on the plane?"

She shook her head. She'd never really liked flying all that much and being inside a stuffy airplane for hours on end with nothing to do hadn't helped.

"Not much," she admitted.

"I'm guessing all you want to do is go home and sleep for the next day or so," Adam replied.

Georgia snorted at her other best friend. One of the things that made her friends so perfect together was that Adam also had the good looks and the height, at almost two metres tall, which would have brought the modelling agencies running, if he had shown the least amount of interest.

Adam had chosen to study medicine instead and was now a resident at Auckland Hospital.

His blue eyes regarded her with concern which from anyone else she would have found disconcerting. She sighed softly.

"I wish I could sleep for the next week," she said. "I have to be at the office at eight tomorrow morning." She groaned, glancing at her watch. It was almost five now. How her boss expected her to be back on deck so early, not even giving her time to get over her jet lag, she didn't know.

She told them about the man on the plane, then remembered the other man she had seen in the terminal.

"Oh," she said. "You'll never guess who I saw. Thought I saw."

"Who?" Adam asked.

"Remember Quinn?"

Lacey frowned at her, clearly not remembering. "Quinn who?"

"Quinn Masters. You remember him Adam. Your dad used to work for him."

Adam nodded. "Yeah, I remember. I thought he was in the UK?"

She shrugged. It was obvious Adam knew nothing about the possibility of Quinn coming back to New Zealand. Then again, the subject probably wouldn't have come up in conversation with his father.

"Maybe he decided to come back." Of course, she could have imagined it was him. Given how tired she felt it wouldn't be a stretch to think she was imagining having seen their old friend. "I don't know. Maybe it wasn't him. But he had a teenage girl with him. Wouldn't his daughter be about thirteen now?"

Adam frowned. "Olivia? That was her name, right? Yeah, I guess she would be about that age. Huh."

He grabbed the handle of her suitcase, wheeling it behind him with one hand, while Georgia held on to her other case. Her friend was carrying her laptop.

"You sure it was him?" Lacey asked, holding her son's hand as they started for the exit doors.

"I think so. Unless he has a doppelganger, but ..." She shrugged again, doubting the reliability of her memory.

She looked at Adam as he pulled his car keys out of his pocket.

"Have you spoken with him or had any messages from him?"

Adam shook his head. "We lost touch," he replied.

Georgia nodded. It had been twelve years since Quinn had left for the UK, taking his then nine-month-old daughter with him. It was easy to see how Adam could have lost touch, especially after everything that had happened.

Quinn had been inconsolable when his wife Scarlett had died in a car crash. Georgia had wondered if Quinn had blamed himself for the accident and that was why he couldn't bear to stay. He'd applied for a job in the UK, getting an ancestry visa as his mother's father had been born in England.

It was a short distance from the terminal to the car park. Georgia heard the beeps as Adam deactivated the alarm on his BMW and opened the boot. He lifted Georgia's suitcase and placed it inside, then picked up the smaller case.

Georgia helped her friend with the children, making sure they were secure in their child seats. Normally there would be plenty of room in the back of the car but with two car seats, it made for slightly cramped quarters as Georgia sat behind the driver's seat.

She noticed her friend was quiet as Lacey buckled her own seat belt in the front passenger seat.

"You okay?" she asked.

Lacey turned her head and looked at her, giving her a weak smile.

"I'm fine. Just a little under the weather, I guess."

"She had that stomach flu that's been doing the rounds," Adam put in, getting in and starting the car.

Her friend nodded. "Lucky the kids didn't get it," she said, handing two-year-old John James a soft toy, which he immediately began chewing. Georgia noticed it was one she had knitted for JJ while she was pregnant with her own son, Liam.

Lisa, the couple's daughter, fell asleep in her car seat. Georgia had to fight her own drowsiness, knowing it wouldn't help her jet lag if she went to sleep too early. She had made that mistake once and had missed an important meeting.

By the time her friends dropped her off at her apartment, she could barely keep her eyes open. She managed to stay awake long enough to heat up some soup in the microwave and eat it before falling into bed, not even unpacking her luggage.

www.ingramcontent.com/pod-product-compliance
Lightning Source LLC
Chambersburg PA
CBHW062109170626
46813CB00002B/373

* 9 7 8 0 4 7 3 3 9 6 2 8 2 *